THE
PERILOUS
ROAD

THE
PERILOUS
ROAD

WILLIAM O. STEELE

With an Introduction by Jean Fritz

SCHOLASTIC INC.
New York Toronto London Auckland Sydney

ISBN 0-590-45128-6

Copyright © 1958 by William O. Steele. Copyright renewed 1986 by Mary G. Steele, Mary Quintard Steele, Jenifer Steele Ogus and Allerton William Steele. Introduction copyright © 1990 by Jean Fritz. All rights reserved. Published by Scholastic Inc., 730 Broadway, New York, New York 10003, by arrangement with Harcourt Brace Jovanovich Publishers.

12 11 10 9 8 7 6 5 4 3 2   1 2 3 4 5 6/9

Printed in the U.S.A.   28

First Scholastic printing, October 1991

*To the staff of the
Library of the University of Chattanooga
for favors granted and service rendered,
and now will you be quiet?*

AUTHOR'S NOTE

The Federal Army may or may not have had a mule
corral on Signal Mountain in the latter part of
September, 1863, as I have used it, but certainly
there can be no doubt that the Confederate General
Joseph Wheeler led a devastating cavalry raid on
the Federal wagon train in Sequatchie Valley,
October 2, 1863.

Introduction

The most heartbreaking part of the Civil War was when the first anger, the first heroics, the first dream of a quick victory, were spent and the armies on both sides realized that they were all homesick boys caught up in a struggle they had to see through. Hard as it was to witness the battles, it was even more difficult to watch the two armies in the lulls in between, when they were in shouting distance of each other. This was so in Fredericksburg, where a Yankee soldier would call, "Hey, Johnny Reb, got any tobacco? Want to trade?" And on Christmas Eve, when the Confederate and Union bands spontaneously struck up together "Home, Sweet Home."

Although we know there are many ways of looking at the war, we are one hundred percent for fourteen-year-old Chris Brabson when the Yankees invade his beloved Tennessee hills, taking his family's crops and his father's only horse. All Chris can do is hate, hate, hate. Infuriated when his father points out that Yankees have to eat, too, utterly disillusioned when his older brother, Jethro, signs up with the Union army, Chris feels that no one understands him but Silas Agee, a forty-year-old, rather eccentric friend, with whom he goes hunting and who claims to be a Confederate spy.

Of course Chris, longing as he does body and soul to take revenge on the Yanks, thinks he has found his chance when he sees the valley below filling up with Yankee supply wagons. He runs to tell Silas, who in turn runs off, presumably to report the news to the Confederates so they can take action. At this point William Steele, always a master of adventure, gives his plot its crucial twist: His brother Jethro, Chris discovers, is a wagoner.

So it is love, not hate, that sends Chris barreling into the Yankee camp. He must warn Jethro. Desperately he goes from campfire to campfire asking for him, and on the way he finds out something about Yankees. They are actually human. Likeable, even. There is one, for instance, who is worried that he's not home helping with the hay and one who takes the trouble to bring Chris some ginger snaps. And when the Confederates come and open fire on the wagoners, Chris sees these lonely young men who have befriended him killed and wounded before his eyes. In such a nightmare of destruction, how can there be hate left?

This is a suspense-filled adventure story. It is also a realistic picture of a boy who grows up, not slowly over the years but suddenly in one shattering night. More important, it is a peace story. "Maybe when you git growed up," Chris's father tells him, "folks can think of a better way to settle their differences than shooting at each other."

Mr. Steele not only writes a good story, he writes good history that accurately reflects the feelings, the worries, the dangers of the times. And the language. When he refers to Native Americans as "redskins" or "savages," the reader understands that he finds these terms as objectionable as we do; he is simply recording what his characters would really have said. Only a skillful writer can tell a story that is true to *its* times and wind up with a truth that speaks to *all* times.

—Jean Fritz

THE PERILOUS ROAD

1

I made sure some Yankee soldier had pulled this spring up out of the ground and hauled it off. Chris Brabson panted, pushing through the calico bushes.

He had run most of the way from the cabin, so as not to keep Silas Agee waiting, and he'd thought for a while he had missed the turnoff, familiar as he was with it. But there the spring was, flowing cool and clear from the side of Walden's Ridge.

He leaned his rifle against a tree and dropped to his stomach to drink. The water was good, cold and sweet, freestone water like most of the mountain springs in these parts.

Chris sat up and wiped his mouth. Silas was bound to be here shortly. It wasn't like him ever to be late, especially when they were going squirrel hunting. Chris could wait. It was pleasant to sit in the sun with nothing to do, no beans to shuck, no wood spoon to whittle, no corn-shuck bridle to braid.

The water gurgled past him over the rocks, slid from sight with only a faint murmur. It was soothing to hear, like a soft rain falling on oak shingles. And right where it disappeared, a little purple sweet gum leaned out over the cliff's edge.

Sweet gums and black gums and sourwoods made the woods bright now when oaks and hickories had just begun to look dull and faded. He grinned, gazing about. Late September, with the trees turning and the nuts falling and the weather holding out good, was the best weather in the world for hunting. Oh, nobody liked to hunt in the fall of the year like Chris Brabson.

He looked back up the slope, hoping to see Silas coming. But all he saw were some dark-green pines and gray rocks standing out so plain against the clear blue of the sky it made him catch his breath.

"I wouldn't live nowheres else on God's green earth but here," he said aloud. "Not in Chattanooga where folks live all scrunched up close together in them fine houses, nor in Caroliny where the ocean is, not even in Chiny across the sea."

From the way the circuit rider talked about China, Chris reckoned nobody ever went hunting there— nor saw the sarvis berry bloom in the spring, nor went swimming in the summertime, nor ever ate so much as one roast'n'ear. Oh, right here was the finest place in the world to live, he thought proudly. Nobody else had such sweet spring water or lived high on a mountain over a valley full of blue and purple shadows. Nowhere else in the world did the sky rise so far overhead so deep and blue and cloudless.

An acorn dropped into the spring and bobbed off. Chris threw a stick after it and watched them both disappear. Restlessly he got up and climbed over the rocks to the mountain's edge, carrying his rifle in one hand. Below him lay Sequatchie Valley, a narrow trough full of wooded patches and square fields and wiggly creeks.

Then he saw it! His face hardened. Almost without knowing it, he threw his rifle to his shoulder and aimed at the little trail of dust along the valley road. He could barely make out the tiny dots, but he knew what they were.

"I reckon I was wrong," he muttered, dropping his gun. "Walden's Ridge *used* to be the finest place in creation." But now the Yankee devils had come here and changed all that.

He knew as well as any living soul how mean the Federal soldiers were. He'd never forget that day, not so long as he lived. He remembered how he'd stood around on Anderson Road, waiting and waiting for Silas to come back from Chattanooga. He'd been so proud, he'd been so anxious, he could almost feel the feather-softness of that shirt over his arms and shoulders. A real leather hunting shirt, made out of the smoothest and finest of deerskins.

It had cost him a heap in time and trouble. Chris had shot the deer himself, three of them, so that he could use only the very choicest parts of the skins in the making of his long fringed shirt. And he'd done the skinning, too, though he wasn't the best in the world at it. He had worked slowly and carefully, easing the skin off the way Silas told him to, making sure that no bits of fat were left anywhere.

Then scraping off the hair, that was a job to take the pertness plumb out of a body. He'd spent many a back-breaking hour on it. There wasn't any easy way to do it, for every single smidgen of hair had to come off. He'd scraped and scraped till his fingers were numb and could no longer hold the knife.

Then he and Silas had soaked the hides, rubbing them every day with brains and liver till they were soft and supple as mole-velvet to the touch. Oh, they were beautiful then, and Chris couldn't wait for his shirt. He'd be the onliest body in these parts with so fine a buckskin shirt, that rain couldn't wet, that briers couldn't hang in, that wouldn't ever wear out, hardly.

Silas had cut the shirt out and made the fringes

from the scraps. "But I ain't no hand with a needle," he told Chris. "I'll have to take it down to my sister in Chattanooga and let her piece it together. Less'n you want your mammy to do it."

"Naw," answered Chris. "I don't want Mammy nor Pappy nor Leah nor none of 'em to know nothing about it till I come strutting in with the shirt on. Tell your sister I'd be mighty much obliged if'n she'd do it for me, Silas."

So Silas had gone off with the cut-out shirt, and Chris had waited the longest kind of time for him. "I'll be back in two days," Silas had promised, and Chris thought the hours would never pass. Two days went by, and the biggest part of the third.

And then Silas had come limping down the road with his clothes dusty and a cut across his head, and no hunting shirt.

"The Yanks took it," he told Chris. "If'n I'd had a gun, they wouldn't never have got it. But I didn't have a chance. Four men on horseback they was, and they come along and took all my truck— my little dab of salt I traded for and four eggs my sister give me, and the shirt. Chris, boy, I'll tell you the truth. I'd a heap rather they'd of took my right arm than that shirt."

Chris didn't say a thing. But right then and there

he'd made up his mind. If he ever got a chance, he'd make some Yank pay for this, if he never did another thing.

Now he watched the dust move up the valley below. "I wisht I had me some kind of special long-shooting rifle," he whispered. "I could just stand right here and pick off them Yanks by the dozen."

He wondered what the soldiers were up to. But then he reckoned he knew. They were out raiding and looting the countryside, stealing anything they could lay hands on.

Yankees ain't no better than Injuns, he told himself. *They're meaner than Injuns for a fact.*

Silas said there wasn't an ear of corn or a shoat pig left in the valley. The Union soldiers had stolen them all. For the life of him, Chris couldn't see how folks could favor the Yankees. But some did, some right here on Walden's Ridge. Even Chris's own pappy sometimes spoke up for the Feds. "They're doing their duty the way they see it," he said. "And they got to eat."

They could go home, Chris reckoned. There was food aplenty for them at home. They had no right to come here shoving folks around, taking their food and their hunting shirts.

Chris cupped his hand to shade his eyes, watching the road. *Well, anyhow, they ain't come around our cabin. And they'd better not,* he added. *They come a-prowling around, and I just naturally aim to kill me a few.*

He reckoned an eleven-year-old boy could do that much anyway. Oh, it was terrible hard to be so young when your country needed you. A plague of locusts was on the land, and he couldn't so much as wave his hand to drive them off. He could shoot, he could shoot as well as any man. And he was strong and tough. He ought to be doing something to help the Confederate States win the war. And instead he was at home hoeing corn and fetching up the cows.

Silas said it would take a while to lick the Yanks. Maybe next year Chris could join up. He'd have to slip off. His mammy and pappy were always talking about how they wanted no part in the war. His mammy said, "Blessed are the peacemakers."

And his pappy said, "Brabsons don't own slaves and never did. This is a rich man's war."

But no Yankee soldier had stolen from them yet. They'd sing a different tune if the Feds ever came pushing them around.

A yell behind Chris made him turn, and he saw Silas Agee coming down the slope toward the spring.

Chris grinned to see him sliding on the loose gravel, hollering and taking on like a young 'un instead of a man grown, forty or so years old.

"No need to hurry, Silas," he called. "I done shot every one of the blue-backed varmints."

"I wisht it was so," Silas answered, coming up with him. "There ain't nothing I'd rather do this morning than shoot Yankees, even if the hides don't fetch a penny apiece."

Silas stood still a minute, looking down into the valley.

"I'd give my right arm to keep 'em off the mountain, but there ain't no way to do it," he commented. "I seen a wagon train on Anderson Road this morning, heading toward Chattanooga."

He turned away then and started up the rise. Chris moved close behind him. Suddenly the boy stopped. "There's somebody coming," he told Silas.

They both stood there, waiting. Chris hoped for just a minute it would turn out to be a Yankee soldier. *I'd shoot him,* he told himself. *Shoot him and shove him right off the bluff and wouldn't nobody ever know, just me and Silas, and we wouldn't tell.*

But it wasn't a Federal. It was just an ordinary man on horseback. He drew rein and yelled down at the two hunters. "Is there a spring down there?" he asked. "Can I water my horse?"

"Come along down, stranger," answered Silas. "This here water's sweet as cherry wine."

The man dismounted and led his horse down to the spring. He knelt and drank right along beside the animal. He looked hot and tired.

"You're right," he said. "That's fine water." He stood and wiped his forehead and the back of his neck.

Silas studied the newcomer. "Mister, don't I know you? Ain't you one of them Webbs from back up near Grassy Cove?" he asked at last.

The man nodded. "That's right," he answered. "Jesse Webb is who I be. And I'm beat out. I been riding since yesterday afternoon. I heared my boy was a prisoner in Chattanooga, and I'm headed that way to see can I get a chance to talk to him." He looked at Silas. "How you reckon the Yankees will treat me?"

Silas gave a short laugh. "Like an egg-sucking hound dog," he said.

"You don't think they'll let me in to see my boy after I come all this way?" Jesse Webb asked anxiously.

"I wouldn't put no faith in it," Silas told him.

It was cruel to see the way the man sagged at that. Chris felt sorry for him and wished Silas hadn't been so blunt about it.

"I'm a preacher on Sundays. You reckon that'd make any difference?" Mr. Webb went on hopefully. "I reckon all them locked-up Rebel boys could use a little comfort for the spirit. A jailer would be hardhearted, for a fact, if he wouldn't let a man of God speak to them prisoners."

Silas scratched his chin. "They just might let you in and then again they might not," he said. "Yankees is queer. There ain't no telling which way they'll jump."

The man looked out into the valley. At last he spoke. "I reckon I'll take my chances with the Yankees. I aim to go on." He turned back to Silas. "Is this trail I'm on the best way? I ain't been up here on Walden's Ridge since I was a tad."

"It runs smack into Anderson Road," Silas answered. "And Anderson Road leads east across the mountain and down into Chattanooga. You can't get lost; there's Yankees traveling it all the time."

The horse raised its head and snorted, moving away from the spring. Mr. Webb grabbed at the reins and jerked the animal back. "Yankees!" he repeated. "How come the Yankees are running around loose? Up at Grassy Cove we heared tell General Bragg had them sealed up inside Chattanooga like a frog in a bottle. Has Bragg got 'em or ain't he?"

"Well, now he's got 'em and he ain't got 'em, you might say," Silas answered.

Chris could see the preacher didn't think that was much of a reply, and he himself thought Silas ought to do better than that.

"You ain't never been to Chattanooga?" asked Silas.

Mr. Webb shook his head.

"Well, it ain't going to be easy to explain, with the river and mountains running every which a way," Silas went on. "But General Bragg has surrounded all but the river side of town. The Feds can only come and go across the Tennessee River, and it don't help them none to speak of. Their supplies are at Bridgeport, Alabama. You know where that is?"

The preacher shook his head again. "Walden's Ridge right around here is as fur south ever I been," he said.

"Bridgeport is a good sixty miles from Chattanooga, and the onliest way open for the Yanks to get back and forth between them places is right over Walden's Ridge," Silas said. "Well, it takes two, three days to make the trip from Bridgeport, and the Yanks just ain't got enough mules or wagons to keep all the soldiers in Chattanooga fed. So long as the Feds are fools enough to hold the town, they'll slowly starve to death."

Mr. Webb didn't look like he'd understood a bit of what Silas explained. What Chris couldn't understand was why any town was worth starving for. If he was a Federal general, he'd head quick for Bridgeport where the supplies were.

Silas looked around at Chris and winked. "And you know it just grieves me something terrible," he went on, "to think of them poor Yankee boys in Chattanooga getting thinner and thinner and their ribs a-sticking out pitiful-like." And he threw back his head and laughed. "Bragg's got 'em for sure, 'cause they're too scared to fight since he whipped them at Chickamauga last weekend. They'll have to retreat and give him the town."

The preacher studied that for a moment. He was worried. "If Yankee soldiers don't have no food, then I reckon their prisoners have got even less," he said.

"That's right, I reckon," Silas agreed. He motioned toward Jesse Webb's bulging saddlebags. "And if that's vittles for your boy, he won't never get a chance at 'em. The Feds are starving to death, and they'll eat anything or anybody not too old and tough to chew."

Silas gave a wicked grin. "I been down there once or twice a-trading squirrels," he went on. "Them boys is so hungry, they'll trade a heap of powder and lead for squirrels. Why, the onliest meat they're getting now is what rats they can catch."

Chris felt something hot and sick in his throat. Eating rats! Would you cook the tail or cut it off, he wondered?

Jesse Webb started up the path, pulling the horse along behind him. "This world is a sorry place," he said sadly. "Brother fighting brother, men that have gone to do their duty starving and dying, turned into thieves and murderers by the pale horse of war. Oh, I wisht I'd never lived to see this day."

Silas spoke out cheerfully. "Oh, it's bad times all right, but don't you get downhearted, Brother Webb. Me and Chris here ain't begun to fight yet. And when we do, look out, Yankees, 'cause we're mountain bearcats."

"I aim to join up just as soon as my pa can spare me," Chris said.

The preacher reached the trail and mounted his horse. He looked down the slope, his eyes on Chris. "Son, you stay to home with your mammy and your pappy as long as you're able," he advised. "War ain't nothing but wickedness, and them that live to come home will have the mark of the beast upon them."

He kicked his horse and rode off without looking back.

"Never even said 'Thank ye,' " complained Silas.

"The way he talked, you'd most nigh think he was a Yankee himself," said Chris.

"Preachers just don't understand fighting," Silas told him. "A body has got to fight for what he believes in. And it comes time to join up, you join and help out."

"I aim to," Chris said. "A boy as handy as me with a rifle ought not to have no trouble being a soldier."

"Oh, you'll make a dandy soldier," Silas agreed. "I 'low you wouldn't have no trouble killing Yankees. And that's the best kind of soldier there is, the Yankee-killing ones." He started off. "Come on. We done wasted half the morning gabbing."

They were a good piece down the ridge by noon. They started back, stopping only long enough to divide up the squirrels.

"I'll take these here four shot in the left eye," Silas said quickly, tossing the animals to one side and counting out four others for Chris.

Chris frowned. "Silas, you know that's just an old tale. Them kind don't taste any better than the ones shot somewheres else."

"I know it," Silas admitted sheepishly. "But my pap always said less'n a squirrel was shot in the left eye, the meat wasn't fitten to eat. And they do seem to eat better shot that way." He went on sorting. "Them's yours and these here I'll take and see can I find some Federal willing to give me powder and shot."

Chris nodded. Silas would give him half of what he traded for. And Chris was always glad to get powder. His pappy only gave him the least little bit to go hunting with today.

He picked up his squirrels and shouldered his gun. He was mighty hungry, and he and Silas went along briskly without talking much. He could see smoke rising from his chimney as they topped a rise and started down toward the Brabson clearing.

Suddenly Silas stopped and said softly, "Chris, you got company to your house. And I don't like the way it smells."

Chris looked at him, puzzled. He pushed past Silas to see, and then he almost cried out. The clearing was full of soldiers in blue uniforms—Yankee soldiers!

2

Chris stood watching the soldiers stuff flitches of bacon and middling meat and handfuls of turnips into their saddlebags. He could hardly believe it. He hadn't reckoned the Yankees would ever find their way to his cabin, stuck 'way back in the woods such a long piece from Anderson Road. But there they were, stealing all the Brabsons' food, even loading up his pappy's onliest horse with bags of corn and strings of shucky beans.

Anger swelled up inside his chest so hot and big he couldn't breathe, spread through his body till he thought he'd bust wide open. He hated those blue-coated soldiers so bad all he could think about was hate—hate and how fine it would be to shoot one of the Yankees, to see him lie still in the clearing. He flung aside his squirrels and swung his rifle up.

Silas grabbed him quick. "Whatever ails you, boy?" he grunted.

Chris jerked away and put his rifle to his shoulder. He would shoot one of those scabby-faced, sow-colored Yankees or die trying.

But Silas was after him like a snake. "Quit that!" he snarled. He knocked the gun aside and dug his fingers in the boy's shoulders.

Chris jerked and twisted, trying to squirm away. He kicked angrily at Silas's legs and jabbed at his stomach with his elbow, but the man's fingers squeezed all the harder.

"Leave go, Silas!" Chris panted. "They ain't after your meal and your horse and your seed corn!"

He went right on struggling, and Silas shook him hard, well-nigh snapping his head off his body. It brought him up short, and he stopped still. Silas dragged him along the trail away from the clearing.

"You oughta be bored for the simples!" Silas growled at him. "You shoot now and you're just as liable to kill your own ma as one of them blue boys. And if'n you was to hit one of the Yanks, I reckon them others would kill your folks just to get even. And come after you and kill you, too, like as not. Them's cavalry, and they don't think twice about running them fancy swords right through poor folks like you and me."

Chris wasn't listening. He was remembering all the hot back-breaking hours he'd spent planting and hoeing and working those beans and turnips and corn. And now it had all come to naught. Oh, the Brabsons would be hungry this winter, for a fact. It was all he could do to keep from crying, thinking about it. And it was mortal hard to stand here and see Federal soldiers stealing and not lift a hand to prevent it. What was the matter with the world, that half its people could be so cruel and hateful? It wasn't right.

He gripped his rifle tight with both hands. It was more than human flesh could bear.

"Don't you act up again," Silas warned him. "You do and I swear I'll swat you a master blow."

Chris looked up at him, his eyes filled with fury. "I can't stand letting them get away with all that meanness," he blurted out.

"Hush," Silas said softly. "Don't I know how you feel? And I know a way we can get back at them devils."

Chris felt his heart give a triumphant lurch under his ribs. He was ready for anything.

Silas glanced toward the clearing. Through the

trees Chris could see two of the soldiers mounting their horses. Mr. Brabson stood off to one side, talking with an officer.

"Come along," Silas urged. "They're a-fixing to leave." He stuffed his squirrels into a bush and jogged off down the trail, and the boy followed.

For some time they ran silently through the woods. They startled a deer, and it rose out of the laurel, sun-red in the black leaves. Pine trees stretched up overhead tall as the wind. And everywhere were square blocks of dark hemlocks. Chris felt strange and light-headed. It didn't seem real. The Yankees hadn't really been to his house. None of this was true.

Chris got a stitch in his side and stopped. He wiped his face with his sleeve. It was a powerful hot day to be running at a pace like this. Silas stopped, too. But he didn't have any stitch, Chris could tell. He was hardly breathing deep. Silas was hickory-tough.

"You know Iron Creek Holler?" Silas asked. "The place where your brother Jethro's horse throwed him that time? Well, that's the spot I figured we could ambush these rascals. You get on one side and me on the other. We can get in a couple of shots apiece."

Chris pictured the spot in his mind, how the trail ran beside the creek to the head of the hollow. It was the finest kind of place for an ambush. "You reckon they'll give chase?"

"Naw, I don't reckon so," answered Silas. "They'll be scared to. Just that little handful by themselves up here in the woods. They ain't much for fighting less'n they got a heap of captains and generals around to tell 'em what to do. They'll just hope to get back to camp with all that plunder. They won't fight back."

He paused. "If'n they do, run for the bluffs. That's rough country, and they won't follow far." He looked hard at Chris and asked, "You ain't scared, be you?"

"You know I ain't scared one bit," Chris retorted quickly. "I'd do anything to get even with them low-down critters."

A horse snorted and a man yelled at it. Chris jumped. The Yankees had almost caught up with them. He and Silas would have to burn up the ground. They set out running again, across a gorge, through an oak woods, and at last reached the hollow where the hills on each side crowded close to the trail.

But the soldiers were right behind them, had come on at a trot.

"Quick." Silas panted. "They're mighty nigh on us. Hide in that dog-hobble bush up there."

Chris scrambled up the slope. It was steep and slick with dead leaves. He slid and slipped and finally had to drop down on his hands and knees, pulling himself up by roots and saplings.

When at last he pushed down into the thick leaves of the dog-hobble, the soldiers had reached the hollow. He could hear the squeak of leather and the jingle of spurs above his thumping heart. He was panting so, he'd never be able to steady his rifle. Oh, if Silas just wouldn't shoot yet, give him a chance to get set.

There was the sharp sound of iron hoofs on rock. Chris sat up and peered out. The soldiers were on the trail right beneath him. He tried to bring his rifle up through the hobble, ease it to his shoulder as quick and quiet as possible.

Silas's shot rang out, and Chris all but cried, for he'd not get even one shot at the blue-coats now. The cock of his gun was caught under a twig. He yanked at it angrily, rising up out of the bushes to give it a good tug. There was a heap of noise and confusion on the trail, shouts and yells and whin-nies, but he didn't take time to see what was hap-pening. He jerked his rifle loose and pulled the leaves from under the cock.

He brought his rifle up, unsteady as he was, trying to brace one foot against a rock. For a minute he couldn't make out a thing on the trail. Suddenly a horse reared right below him, and the rider beat at it with his fist, shouting and cursing. Before Chris could fire, the horse and soldier charged off.

The officer was pointing straight at him, screaming, "Get 'em! Get 'em! Up yonder in the bushes."

There was another shot, but Chris didn't know whether it was Silas again or one of the Yanks shooting at him. His foot was sliding off the rock, but there was no time to worry about that. His rifle was wobbling all over the place. Quickly he pulled the trigger, and the gun roared in the hollow. He fell backwards into the bushes, not knowing whether he'd hit anything or not. A horse screamed, and the officer kept on shouting.

Chris grabbed the dog-hobble and pulled himself over on his knees. Digging his toes into the soft earth, he struggled up the rest of the slope. They were already coming after him. He could hear the heavy breathing of the horses.

They won't make it up that hillside, he told himself. *It's like trying to climb a peeled slippery elm.*

But he was wrong. He hadn't more than reached the top before the horses came up a little to the right of the way he'd made it. *They must of found a draw or something*, he thought. *I made sure horses couldn't get up there.*

He ran then, for a fact. He wasn't a coward, but he'd heard a heap of tales about cavalrymen, and all of them were fierce. Silas had been right about those swords.

But Silas had been wrong about the rough country discouraging the Yankees. Chris was the one who was getting discouraged. He ran over rocks and down gullies and through laurel tangles, but he couldn't seem to shake off the horsemen. He was tired to the bone, and a great fiery pain throbbed in his side. But he wouldn't give up.

He stumbled and fell to his knees. Gulping air, he crouched there a minute, trying to think. What in creation was he going to do? He glanced around, feeling like a cornered rat. He could hide in some laurel slick, but he misdoubted they'd be hard put to find him. He could climb a tree but not these big old trees with their lowest limbs out of reach over his head.

He heard his pursuers coming, and he got up and trotted off along the edge of the mountain, his feet stumbling over every root and rock. He couldn't keep up this running. He'd been going hard since sunup this morning, and he was plumb beat out.

He staggered wearily on through the bushes and around boulders and finally came out onto the flat top of a bluff. He knew he'd have to give up. He'd run his last bit; he couldn't take another step. With trembling hands Chris loaded his rifle. He would fight for his life, get in one shot anyway before he was run down and hacked to pieces.

Then he saw the great crack at the side of the bluff, a place where the rock had split apart. He ran over to it and looked down. There were enough cracks and grab-holds for him to climb down. He could hide there out of sight of the soldiers. He'd have to be mighty quick though.

There was a long drop to the bottom of the split and the wickedest-looking rocks in all creation right under him. It gave him a queer, clutching feeling in his stomach, and he drew back.

But I ain't got no choice, he told himself. *It's my onliest chance.*

Quickly he hid his rifle among the bushes, covering it with dead leaves. Then he dropped to the edge and squirmed over, holding on to a little twisty pine. His toes found a crack in the rock, and he let go the pine tree and dropped from sight. He grabbed a rough knob and lowered himself still farther down the cliff.

He heard the soldiers coming then. The horses' iron shoes clanged on the rock. He cowered in his hiding place. They were almost on top of him. They'd see him sure if he didn't edge down a little more. He shifted his body and crouched a little, reaching for a handhold.

But he reached too far. For a minute he clung to the wall, and then his feet slipped off the tiny ledge below him. He was falling!

3

Chris clawed frantically at the cliff, scrabbling about for a foothold, grabbing at any crack, anything at all. His body slithered down the rough surface. He was as good as killed, headed straight down for those jagged rocks. He'd end up a heap of broken bones and bleeding meat, too dead to skin.

His hands raked over the ledge he'd been standing on, and he grasped it desperately. The weight of his body almost jerked his fingers loose, but there he hung with his face pressed against the rock. Chris shut his eyes tight. He knew in reason he couldn't hold on here long.

He almost cried out. He had to shut his jaws tight so he wouldn't yell and grind his teeth together to keep himself from begging the soldiers to pull him up. He was scared of dying but not so scared that he'd ask help of a Yankee. Never!

I'd sooner ask a rattlesnake, he thought, and he gripped the rock edge for all he was worth.

Over his head one of the soldiers spoke. Chris could hardly hear what he said, the horses were making such a racket, pawing at the rock and snorting around.

"He's gone. Got away from us slick as a snake going down a hole."

The other soldier laughed. "I expect these mountain folks know holes around here even the snakes don't know about," he answered. "You know, I wouldn't mind living here myself. I've never in my life seen a finer sight than this view."

Go away, go away, go away, Chris prayed silently. His fingers were getting numb. *Don't let them blue-coats be here when I drop. Make 'em go away.*

"View!" The first man grunted scornfully. "There ain't no view fine enough to make me want to live in this Godforsaken country. Why, the folks around here are ignorant as skinned mules. Give me flat country where people have got some sense."

He wheeled his horse and rode off. After a moment the other soldier went after him.

Come back! cried Chris. *Oh, come back and pull me up. It's all your fault I'm a-hanging here about to die.*

But he didn't cry it aloud. He only said it inside his head. He wouldn't ask these Yankee soldiers for so much as a crumb of help. He couldn't think of words wicked and vile enough to say about them. For a minute he hated them so much he forgot about his hands hurting, forgot he was hanging on a cliff high above Sequatchie Valley.

They were gone. There wasn't even the echo of a hoofbeat, only the wind sighing along the bluff's edge. He was alone with only a few minutes left to live. His hands ached like they'd been frostbitten, and his arms were about to pull out of the joints. Sweat ran down his face and neck.

His fingers slipped a mite on the edge. Hard as he tried, he couldn't make them keep their grip. Oh, he knew how this kind of thing happened! No matter how hard a body tried, he got so tired his muscles wouldn't do what he told them to. In a spell now his hands would give way, would lose their hold in spite of all his efforts. He would fall then.

He wished he'd been able to say good-bye proper to his mammy. He loved his mammy. He wished he'd been able to see her just one more time, to tell her . . .

Somebody was coming!

He could hear somebody singing and hear foot-steps on the bluff. He was going to be saved, but he'd have to holler. Even if it was a Yankee, Chris knew he'd never in this world keep himself from yelling this time.

He opened his mouth to shout, and no sound came out—not so much as a squeak. The footsteps were closer and the singing louder. Whoever it was would go on by and never know that under his feet Chris Brabson hung by his fingertips in the direst kind of peril. He swallowed and worked his tongue around inside his dry mouth.

> "Come all ye fair damsels, take
>   warning from me.
> Never place your affections on a green
>   willow tree;
> For the leaves they will wither like
>   flowers in the spring
> While the waters are a-gliding and the
>   nightingales sing."

He could hear the song plain now. He knew that voice. Jethro! It was his brother Jethro singing a tune!

"Jethro!" Chris cried. This time he did it, but his voice was hoarse and not near loud enough to carry above his brother's singing.

Jethro hit a low note and paused in his song.

Chris filled his lungs with air and shrieked, "Jethro, help!" Oh, his brother had better hurry. He closed his eyes and tried to put all his strength into his fingers to make them hold on just a little longer.

"Chris!" Jethro breathed from overhead.

Chris opened his eyes then and looked up. When he saw his brother leaning down to him, he went limp as a rag. He almost let go and dropped, with help not four feet away from him.

Jethro must have seen he was in a bad way, for he didn't waste time asking questions, just climbed down the crack and grabbed Chris and hoisted him up safe to the top of the bluff.

Chris lay there, curled up like a drowned grub worm. He couldn't say a word, and his arms stretched out before him like two dead sticks, no good to him whatsoever. He was scratched from running through the bushes, and his bare toes had been scraped and rubbed raw where he'd tried to find a toehold in the cliff. And he reckoned he'd never get both feet off the ground again without remembering how he'd felt there on the cliffside, alone and helpless, with nothing to stand on but a heap of empty air. He shuddered all over and sat up.

Jethro rubbed his hands and arms with quick strokes till they didn't ache so bad. Chris was breathing easier now.

"Here," Jethro said, handing over his hat. "I got these here pawpaws for Sallie Jean. But you look like you need 'em the worse way."

The pawpaws were sweet and juicy. They tasted wonderful to Chris's dry mouth and throat. No wonder Sallie Jean liked them so well. Right after she and Jethro were married, she'd planted a heap of pawpaw seeds near where they were building their cabin, Chris remembered. But he didn't reckon the trees were old enough to bear fruit yet. He ate three, spitting the flat brown seeds out over the mountainside.

"Now tell me how in the nation you come to be in a predicament like that?" Jethro asked.

The boy's eyes grew dark with anger. "Did you know the Yankees had been to our house?" he asked. "They done stole everything, all our food and old Codger and the chairs and table and beds, like as not. They aim to starve us to death."

"I reckon you'll make out," said Jethro briefly. "But that don't tell how come you to be hanging over the edge of Walden's Ridge that-a-way. The Yankees never put you there."

"I reckon they did just that," Chris answered sulkily. "Leastways it was their fault I was there. Me and Silas was out squirrel hunting. And when we come home, we seen the Yanks at the cabin, going off with the turnips and corn and meat." He stopped and gritted his teeth. Every time he thought about it he got mad all over again.

"Go on," urged Jethro.

"Well, me and Silas cut out across the woods to Iron Creek Holler and laid wait for 'em," said Chris. "Oh, it was the finest kind of place for an ambush, Jethro. But I didn't have time to get hid good, and when Silas fired, they seen me and come after me. I run, but I couldn't shake 'em. They chased me out on the bluff here, and I aimed to make a stand and fight. And then I seen that crack. I figured I could hide in it. But I slipped getting down in it, and if you hadn't come along, I reckon the buzzards would be picking me up about now."

"I reckon they would at that," said Jethro slowly. "And you wouldn't have deserved no better, falling in with one of Silas's wild schemes."

Chris was surprised. "I never figured you'd talk that way about Silas," he interrupted. "Silas is a good hunter. I reckon he's the best hunter anywhere in these parts. I think a heap of him."

Jethro gave him a look. "I reckon Silas is a mighty fine hunter," he agreed. "But that's all there is to him. He's a fly-by-night. He always likes to have something to be against. Right now he's against the Federals, but he don't rightly take it serious. It's just somebody to take his meanness out on."

Chris sprang up. "You'd ought to be ashamed, Jethro Brabson!" he yelled. "Silas was taking up for your mammy and pappy and brother and sister that the Yankees was a-stealing from. Maybe you didn't break your back over that corn and them turnips. But I did. Maybe you didn't see how proud Mammy was over that smoked side meat she had saved back. But I did. And I wasn't feared to try to shoot the blue-backed mud puppies that stole it, nor Silas neither."

Jethro looked at his brother soberly. "Chris, maybe you didn't know it, but this country's at war. Them soldier boys has got to get food somehow. They can't raise it. If they didn't take it, the Rebels would. Folks on Walden's Ridge won't starve. They may go without, but they won't starve."

"I'd a heap rather the Rebs had it," said Chris. He went over and pulled his rifle out from under the laurel bushes.

Jethro grinned. "So you aimed to stand and fight," he repeated. "Just you against the United States Cavalry."

"I'd have killed one of 'em anyway," Chris muttered fiercely.

"Where was the Yanks when you was hanging off the bluff?" asked Jethro. "How come they didn't pull you up?"

"They was right here," burst out Chris. "Ain't I told you I was hiding from them? Did you think I was going to holler out and let 'em know where I was? It ain't easy to die falling off a bluff, but I misdoubt it's any easier to get cut up by them swords."

Jethro's blue eyes widened. "You mean you was hanging there, with nothing between you and breaking your fool neck, all the time the Federals was looking for you? And you never hollered out?" He laughed a little. "I never heared the like."

"I don't care," the boy said defiantly. "I hate them Yankees. I'd rather die than take help from them."

Jethro was silent a minute, studying his brother. "Well, that's too bad," he said finally, "for you just did."

Chris stared. "What do you mean?" he asked. "What?"

Jethro picked up the hat full of pawpaws. "I mean I'm on the Union side," he told him quickly. "I aim to join the Federal army."

Chris went on staring. For a minute he had again that dizzy, light-headed feeling that nothing was real. And then he turned and ran blindly off into the woods.

"I reckon I should take off this here ring whilst I'm a-digging," Leah said, holding up her small grubby hand. "Ain't it pretty, Chris?"

She turned her hand this way and that, admiring the ring carved from a peach seed and polished to a gleam. "Hit's got such a shine to it."

Chris gave her a disgusted look. "I'd as soon wear chicken gut around my finger as something give me by some old Yankee," he muttered and went back to grubbing in the dusty earth.

A peach-stone ring was mighty poor pay for the food the Yanks had carried off. Last night Chris had come home late, and his mammy had told him the bad news. He hadn't let on he knew a thing, just swallowed his cold vittles without a word. He could see his mammy was tired out and worried enough. And Leah might hop around like a toad-frog bragging about her ring, but Chris had gone to bed thinking now his mammy and pappy knew the truth about Yankee soldiers and their meanness.

Only it hadn't worked out so. In the morning Jethro came over to say he was going to the Union army the next day. A body might think then Mammy and Pappy would speak out, would say nay to their oldest son joining up with such thieves and scalawags.

But they hadn't. And Leah had giddied around yelling about her ring till Chris could have smacked her good and hard.

"It was a real nice man give it to me. He said I was pretty, just real pretty," she went on dreamily now. "I reckon I am. I reckon I'm as pretty as Belle Trantham or Lucy Mai Willis. A heap prettier maybe even. I wisht I had me a blue dress and a yellow sash. Oh, I'd be the prettiest gal in Tennessee, I know in reason."

"You better hush up that kind of foolish talk and get to grabbling up them 'taters," Chris snarled at her. "If'n we don't find more than this, you won't be pretty come the end of winter. You'll be dead. And a skeleton don't look pretty no matter how many yellow sashes it's a-wearing."

Leah took off the ring and stuck the end of her

yellow braid through it. She pulled it way up and then tied the braid in a knot below it. She began to dig in the loose earth with her hands.

"I done found one," she cried after a minute.

Chris looked up. The potato Leah held up was hardly bigger than a walnut. Only a few days ago the two of them had dug up a heap of the finest kind of potatoes, fat and brown and firm, a whole wagonload of them, it seemed to Chris. They'd put them in a bin in the corner of the smokehouse, enough to last all winter. The smokehouse had looked mighty fine then, bacon on the rafters, potatoes and dried apples and turnips everywhere. But the Yanks had taken it all, even the potatoes that had begun to sprout. Now Chris and Leah were out here rooting around like a couple of razorback hogs, hoping to find any little withered potatoes they might.

Oh, them blue-bellies! Chris crumbled dirt clods angrily. *I wisht I had one here right now*, he thought. *I'd squeeze him to pieces. And I ain't going to miss a turn doing something hurtful to the Yankees*, he assured himself.

But he didn't know just what he could do. That was the worst part of it. He couldn't think of anything bad a lone boy could do to the Federals. He wished he could go to Bridgeport, Alabama, and blow up the supply depot there. But he couldn't. Not by himself, anyway. Silas could do it. Maybe he and Silas could do it together.

For the first time, Chris wondered about Silas. He knew in reason Silas had escaped yesterday; he was too slick to get caught. But would Silas tell how he and Chris had fired on the Federals and gotten chased? Or would he think it best to keep quiet about it? Well, the Brabsons would know about it quick enough. Jethro would tell them, Chris reckoned, or they'd find out somehow. There wasn't much that happened on Walden's Ridge folks didn't find out sooner or later and pass on to others.

He sure didn't aim to tell, howsomever. He hadn't opened his mouth, though the muscles in his arms and shoulders were so sore and tight he could almost hear them twang when he worked.

Chris and Leah had almost finished going over the potato patch when Mrs. Brabson came out of the house. She poked at the heap of wizened potatoes with her toe. "Them fellers is mighty puny, ain't they?" she remarked. "We won't hardly git two meals out of them."

"We'll starve, I reckon," said Leah cheerfully.

"Leastways, Chris says we'll starve afore spring. I reckon I'll make a bee-yootiful corpse. Mammy, you bleach my winding sheet white as white and give me some white flowers to hold, some of them windflowers that bloom down by the creek. I reckon I'll make such a pretty corpse folks will come from miles around to see me laying in my bury box."

"Now, hush," cried Mrs. Brabson. "It ain't decent to talk so, Leah. A body eight years old ought to know that!"

She frowned and rubbed her palms together. "And we ain't fixing to starve. We still got a dab of corn the soldiers missed in that old field down near the spring. And we got the cow, thank goodness. And just last evening I seen one of our hogs in the woods, and she's got three young 'uns with her."

"We'll never catch them, wild as they be," said Chris.

"Well, I guess you can shoot that old sow," Mrs. Brabson told him. "Same as you and your pa can shoot us some game to meat us this winter. There's been a heap of deer tracks around the garden lately. And, Chris Brabson, I just reckon you forgot about chestnuts and scaly-barks and beechnuts a-lying out in the woods a-waiting to be picked up, not to mention persimmons and pawpaws."

"Game'll eat them nuts up afore you even find them," Chris muttered.

"No," Mrs. Brabson went on firmly. "Them boys was hungry. I don't grudge them food. We won't be the first ones ever had to do without 'taters and cornbread and shucky beans."

Chris watched her. Maybe she didn't grudge the food, but she was worried a heap. He could tell she was worried, the way she rubbed her hands together. She always did that when she was fretting, like the time Leah had the ingrowing hives so bad.

"It's the horse," she burst out at last. "There wasn't no sense in them taking old Codger. They'll ride him to death in two days. And your pa'll never get everything done without the horse, the logs snaked up and everything. And however are we going to get the plowing done, just you and me and your pappy and no horse?"

Chris didn't say a thing. He just went on scratching around for potatoes. But he couldn't help being a little mite pleased, just a little bit set up that his mammy knew what bad times were really ahead of them. And oh, it was good as eating butter and honey for him to hear her come right out and say that the Yanks were the ones that had brought this trouble on them. His pappy and Jethro might think the blue-bellies were a band of angels, but his mammy *knew*.

Then he felt downright ashamed of himself, thinking such things. Wasn't it proof of how mean the Yankees were that they could make a boy rejoice to see his very own mammy worried and anxious and hard-put? Oh, there hadn't been a happy day on this mountain since the first of those blue-coated devils had set foot on the trail here.

Mrs. Brabson sighed. "Well, what's done's done. There ain't no use a-bawling over it," she told them. "It's the Lord's will, I reckon. We'll get along. We always have. Come along now, I'll help get these 'taters dug."

All three of them worked and finished up the patch. Chris put the potatoes in a poke and was toting them to the smokehouse when he saw his pappy. Mr. Brabson was skirting the edge of the big field, walking slow and easy, the way he always did. Nobody would know to see him he was in deep trouble.

He came through the trees toward the cabin. Chris opened the smokehouse door and set the sack inside. His mammy always said Pappy had second sight. He knew when there wasn't any use planting a field because drought or blight would get the crop. He knew when folks were coming to visit or the cow was going to be plagued with sickness.

Chris didn't know if it was true. His pappy was so shut-mouthed and secret, a body hardly ever knew what he was thinking. You'd have reckoned, though, if Mr. Brabson could see into the future, he'd have seen how the Yanks were coming to take all their turnips and corn, how all the hard work of planting and hoeing and harvesting were going to waste.

Chris shut the smokehouse door and walked to the spring. It was cool and dim under the big trees. Some little ferns still grew green around the water's edge. Way down deep he could see a crawdad lying on the sandy bottom, just barely floating back and forth when the water flowed past him.

He leaned over and dipped a hand in the spring. The crawdad scurried away. Chris drank and then washed his hands in the cold water.

Maybe his pappy had known. Maybe he planned all along for the Yanks to have all those potatoes and beans and roasting ears Chris had helped raise. Mr. Brabson favored the Yanks. Anybody could see he favored them. He hadn't even raised his voice to try to stop Jethro from joining the Union army.

"If'n I ever find out it's so," said Chris aloud, "if'n I ever find out he let me work myself to the bare bone for them greasy Feds, I'll . . . I'll . . ." He broke off, so angry he couldn't think what he would do.

He looked down and saw his red and twisted face reflected in the spring. For a minute he didn't know who it was glaring up at him, so ugly and full of hate.

And then his heart knotted up with misery. Oh, why couldn't Jethro and his folks see how mean these Yankees were, how they had brought such meanness with them that a boy could get to hate his very own father?

5

The others were already eating when Chris got back to the cabin. There was stew made of the squirrels Chris had shot and cold ash bread left from yesterday's noon meal.

"Savor that bread," said Mrs. Brabson. "It's the last you'll get for a good spell. I got a little dab of meal left, but I ain't aiming to use it till we get the corn out of that field and get it ground."

"It'll have to wait," Mr. Brabson said. "Me and Chris got to snake up them logs just by ourselves, and that'll take time. If'n we don't start now, cold weather will catch us."

Mrs. Brabson frowned. "Couldn't nobody lend you a horse? If'n you had one just for a day, it would sure be a blessing."

"I told you nobody's got a horse," answered Mr. Brabson shortly. "I been all around the barn and back this morning, walked a right smart piece. The

Yanks been everywhere before me. Leastways, that's what folks said. I kind of figger some of 'em still have a mule or horse hid out somewheres, but they was feared to bring it out and lend it. Can't blame folks for that."

He smiled suddenly. "There's a heap of mules around here though, for a fact. The Federals have fenced in a piece of ground on the Sawyer Road and got it plumb full of mules. Leastways, Silas says they have."

"Whatever for?" asked Leah. "Can't they let 'em run wild like we do our stock?"

Mr. Brabson shook his head. "They have to have them handy for the supply wagons coming from Bridgeport. This haul up the mountainside is tarnal hard on critters, and when they get to the pen, they leave the tired mules and get some fresh ones for the rest of the way to Chattanooga."

Mrs. Brabson set down her noggin of sassafras tea. "Well, I reckon a heap of folks will be trying to get theirselves a free mule from there," she remarked. "The ones that had to give their beasts to the Yankees are bound to try to steal one of them mules."

"Oh, that's the Bible truth." Mr. Brabson nodded. "But the Feds ain't aiming to let 'em, I don't reckon. Silas said they got soldiers guarding the place all the time. They'll shoot at anybody who's got no business around there."

Chris ate his ash bread slowly, slowly, but he hardly even tasted it. How come Silas to know so much about what the Yanks were doing? You'd think the hunter would want to stay as far away from them as he could get, after yesterday's fight.

Chris was hardly up from the table when his father loaded him down with chains and a leather harness. Then they set out after the winter's firewood. They cut through the fallow field back of the cabin. Purple ironweed stood up tall and bright above the goldenrod and horseweed, and bunches of black pokeberries dangled from thick crimson stalks.

His pappy had aimed to put that empty field to corn in the spring, but he hadn't gotten around to it. Chris was glad. *I hoed corn enough for them blue-bellies to run off with,* he thought, *without them getting this field full too.*

It wasn't so much the thought of going hungry that made him so rip-staving mad. There was a heap of times a body had to do without. What made him mad was that the Yanks could come swaggering in and take what they wanted and nobody raise a hand. You'd have thought his pappy would try to stand up for his rights. These soldiers didn't belong here; it wasn't their land. It filled him with outrage to think of the soldiers taking the Brabson food like it was theirs, all fair and square, like folks had nothing better to do but sweat all summer long in the fields to feed these thieving outlanders—or hunt the winter through to make shirts for their backs.

A catbrier scratched his leg where his homespun breeches were too short. He slashed at it savagely with the chain and kept on after his father.

They reached the place where the logs lay. There was a power of them. He and Pappy had felled them last February, just before the sap ran up in them. Now they were well seasoned and would burn like paper.

Chris slipped the wide leather strap over his head and fitted it across his chest. Looking at the pile of logs, he groaned to himself. They'd never done this without old Codger, and it seemed to him a man and a boy could hardly do the work of a horse.

Mr. Brabson pointed at one of the logs, and Chris went to it. He worked the chain tied to his leather strap under the log and fastened it. He pulled, testing his harness.

Mr. Brabson stood up and tried his chain harness, too. A July fly hollered overhead, the long hot buzzing sound that always made Chris feel hotter than he was.

"You ready?" asked Mr. Brabson.

Chris nodded and leaned hard against the leather strap. Behind him the chain tautened, and the weight of the log made him take a step backward.

"Wait, Chris," cried Mr. Brabson. "You pulled too soon."

"You said was I ready?" Chris reminded him sulkily.

"Well, you never said was you. Next time, wait till I holler," Mr. Brabson instructed.

Chris slid his eyes around at his father and then stood there, sullen and silent. The September heat rose up from the cleared space. Sweat trickled down his temples and his neck; the choking smell of dust filled his nose and mouth.

"Now, Chris, pull!" called Mr. Brabson, and Chris pulled, leaning his full weight against the leather band and straining hard. He dug his toes into the soft earth, and the log moved jerkily forward. He could hear his father's heavy breathing beside him as they headed down the path toward the cabin. The log slid better on the hard dirt, but Chris had to push through the weeds and vines on his side of the trail. Bushes slapped him in the face, vines caught in his clothes, and dead leaves and twigs showered down on him.

By the time they had reached the clearing, the leather band had rubbed a raw place under his left arm. *One log moved and we been most nigh an hour getting it here,* he thought bitterly. Codger could have brought up two logs, maybe three, while they were getting this one here. At the rate he and Pappy were going, cold weather would be here before they'd even got the wood to the clearing. And then they'd still have to chop the wood into kindling and backlogs.

And his pappy had never even made a fight to save the horse yesterday. Just gave up, happy as a redbird, and handed Codger over to the Yankees. For the life of him, Chris couldn't understand it. And Jethro! What would make Jethro want to throw in his lot with such hateful folks? And how could his mammy and pappy stand it, to know that in a few days Jethro would be wearing a blue uniform and going about robbing honest men?

Sweat trickled into the raw place under Chris's arm and stung like a hornet's bite. "Come on, Pappy," he snarled. "Let's go get another one."

This time he pulled so hard he thought his muscles were going to split. A red haze swam in front of his eyes, and his heart jumped like a rabbit in a snare. He fought the harness as though it was the entire Union army.

"Here, Chris, don't try to pull the whole thing by yourself," cried Mr. Brabson. "It'll be a heap easier on both of us, do we pull together."

Chris stumbled to a halt with his head reeling. Oh, he wished he was a soldier, he wished he could fight, he wished he could do anything to get rid of all the hate bottled up in his innards.

"Take it easy," Mr. Brabson told him. "You'll give yourself a fever working like that in this heat."

Chris stood there panting, the chains clanging around his bare feet. He wouldn't mind having a fever. He wished he would have one and die of it, so he wouldn't have to live in a world where every single thing went wrong.

They went on working. The third log was no more than started along the path when Chris stepped on a thorn. He hopped over into the trail, and the log slid across the top of his foot, scraping the skin raw.

"Dang it!" he shouted and flung off the harness. "I ain't going to do no more," he gasped. "Like as not, when we get them logs up to the cabin, you'll give them to the Yanks. I reckon you think more of them Yanks than you do of anybody. And Jethro!" His voice rose to a howl. "How can a body turn against his own flesh and blood that-a-way? Ain't he always lived here? Ain't this always been a good place? How come he wants to be a traitor?"

He caught his breath. He was shaking all over. He knew he ought to shut up. But somehow he couldn't seem to stop now he was started. "How come you didn't stop Jethro? I reckon you'll be proud of him when he goes around robbing folks the way them Feds done us!"

He quit then. Something about the way his pappy was looking at him made him know he'd gone too far. And for one moment he thought his father was going to slap him good and hard. He braced himself for the blow. Let him. Chris didn't care. He wouldn't be on the Union side, not even if his pappy whipped him half to death for it.

"That'll be enough of that," Mr. Brabson snapped. "Now you listen here to me. I don't want no more talk about Jethro. It took a heap of praying and wrestling before Jethro made up his mind to go, and it ain't for any impudent boy like you, green as a summer pumpkin, to speak out against him. You hold your tongue from now on."

Chris dropped his eyes. He didn't know his pappy could look so fierce.

"It most nigh ain't bearable to see all our hard work gone for naught," Mr. Brabson went on, sounding less stern. "I don't like them Union soldiers shoving in here like that no more than you do. And if I could of kept old Codger, I'd of done it. But I couldn't. There wasn't any way I could save the horse or the food either. And you know it."

Chris glared at the ground. There must have been some way, instead of bowing and scraping and all but kissing the ground them Yankees walked on. Oh, his pappy needn't talk like that to him! Chris had seen what went on, he'd seen just how his pappy handed everything over without so much as a murmur. A body oughtn't to stand there meek as Moses while the soldiers stole food and horses. Chris would have set the smokehouse on fire so the Yanks couldn't have the bacon and turnips. He would have scattered the cornmeal to the four winds before he'd let it go to feed the Federal soldiers.

"It's a bad time," said Mr. Brabson, and his voice was sad. "A civil war like this one is the worst thing can happen to folks, I reckon. The way I see it, war ain't doing nothing but making things worse. I don't hold with slavery. And I surely think the Union ought to hang together. But sending soldiers down here to burn and rob and kill don't seem to me anything but a sin. Can't nothing come of it but more hating and more wickedness."

Then how come you didn't tell them soldiers? cried Chris silently. *How come you didn't show them somehow you thought they was wicked?*

"We're the kind of folks always gets the short end of things in wartime," Mr. Brabson went on.

"And I don't know one thing a body can do about it but grin and bear it."

Chris drooped his shoulders. He didn't stand a chance. Jethro could go off and join the enemy, and that was all right. But he, Chris, couldn't even say what he thought without getting fire and brimstone from his pappy.

"Anyway, there's work to be done, war or no," Mr. Brabson remarked. "Let's get this log a-moving."

Chris felt so dull and beat-out he didn't think he could manage the long haul to the clearing. But he did it. He tried not to think about the Yanks or Jethro or anything but pulling.

"Looky there," cried Mr. Brabson. "We got company. How come Mammy not to blow the horn for us, reckon?"

Chris looked up. Lukie Trantham and his daddy were standing by the cabin door. His mammy was with them, and she looked mad and flustered. Mr. Brabson went over to them. But Chris took off his harness and sat down on the log there at the edge of the clearing, tired as a dog. Whatever was going to happen, it didn't look like it was going to be anything good. He'd stay out of it. He'd had all the trouble he could stand for a spell.

"Howdy, Trantham," called out Mr. Brabson. "Light and set."

Mr. Trantham looked at him coldly. "I never come to no play-party," he said at last. "I come for my saw." And he spat a long spit.

"Your saw?" repeated Mr. Brabson.

He stopped still, and Chris could see the angry color creep up the back of his neck. Oh, his pappy might have known. As soon as it got about that Jethro had gone to the Federals, a heap of people would be bound to turn against the Brabsons. Tranthams were hot Rebels. It stood to reason they wouldn't want folks on the Union side using their saw.

"I'll fetch it," Mr. Brabson said, and his voice was like the ring of an ax on a cold morning. He went toward the shed, and Mr. Trantham and Mammy stood side by side, not looking at each other, not speaking.

But Lukie sidled away through the bushes till he came close to Chris. Chris knew he was there, but he didn't turn to see.

"Blue-belly!" sneered Lukie in a low voice.

Chris winced. He and Lukie used to be good friends. They'd had a heap of fine times together.

"Yankee-lover," said Lukie.

Chris sprang up. It wasn't any use. He couldn't

keep the way he felt shut up inside his chest. He had to speak out or strangle on the words.

"I ain't no such," he snarled. "I hate them sour-face Yanks! I ain't no more a Yankee than you are!"

"Jethro's done joined up with them." Lukie grinned. "Blood's thicker than water, I 'low."

"I don't care what Jethro's done," Chris shrilled wrathfully. "If'n a Yank was to come along now and I had my rifle-gun, I'd shoot him dead!"

"*If'n*," jeered Lukie. "*If'n* never skinned no deer. If you ain't no Fed, prove it."

Chris took a deep breath. "All right, I'll prove it. I'll sure prove it, if'n you're willing to come along and see me do it."

"Oh, I'll come," said Lukie. "Any time's all right with me, for I don't reckon you aim to do anything."

"You be at the Holly Spring on Anderson Road tomorrow night, and I'll prove it a hundred times over," Chris told him. "Less'n you're scared to come."

"Come along, Lukie," bellowed Mr. Trantham. "I'm a-leaving."

Lukie slid off between the bushes. "I'll be there," he called back softly. "I won't be scared. I ain't no blue-belly!"

6

The clearing was fiery with sunset when Chris stepped away from the cabin. His pappy was sitting in the dogtrot smoking, and his mammy was redding up the room after the evening meal. They paid him no mind, but Leah came trailing after him.

"Where you going?" she asked.

"I'm a-going after something," he answered sharply.

What made Leah be such a nuisance? Most times she never bothered her head over him, but let him be doing something he didn't want her to know about, and she was after him like a duck on a June bug.

"What?" cried Leah, running along behind him. "What're you going after, Chris?"

"Laroes to catch medlars," he told her, hurrying on down the path.

"That don't mean nothing," she said, catching

at his shirt. "Chris, you know that don't mean nothing."

"Hit means you'd better git back to the house and leave me alone," snarled Chris, turning on her threateningly. "I don't have to get your leave to walk down the path a piece. Now let me be, or I'll tell the crawdads to come pinch your braids off in the night time."

Leah put her hands quickly up to her hair and held on to her braids tightly. She was almost sure Chris couldn't do this, but she still didn't dare find out. She was proud of those long butter-yellow pigtails. She stared after him as he walked off through the trees.

He left the Brabson place and took the path to Anderson Road. He was uneasy. It wasn't like he was used to going out on this kind of devilment. He tried to walk along careless-like, whistling a little between his teeth and kicking at the scattered pine cones, as though he wasn't going any place special or fretting about anything out of the way.

But it was hard. Every leaf crackling gave him a prickle up his spine, and when he came to Anderson Road, he looked carefully both ways before he stepped out in the open. He hadn't gone ten steps in the wagon ruts before he stopped. He could see a black shape up ahead of him crouching on the side of the road. It was too big for a man. And then he smelled an almighty stink. Whatever it was, it was past harming a body.

It was a mule. He figured it must have been dead quite a spell. Died right in its tracks while it was pulling one of the Federal supply wagons to Chattanooga, he reckoned. Now wasn't that just like the Yanks to work their beasts till they dropped? He held his nose and ran past the dark heap.

In the eastern sky before him a whole handful of stars were out. And a bat twirled and tilted across the road. He padded on through the soft dust. It was powerful dry; there'd been no rain for a month. Behind him the sun's last light was dark crimson in the sky. He rounded a bend and the light was gone, and the dark trees on either side moved in closer. A katydid rasped out, stopped, went steadily on.

The road wound back and forth across the mountaintop. Sometimes ahead of him the moon swam, round and pure and pale in the smoky sky, and then again the tall oaks blotted it from sight. He was getting close to Holly Spring.

Something moved in the shadow of the elderberry bushes, and he slowed his steps. Was it Luke? It looked like somebody bigger than Luke. Things seemed a heap different in the twilight than they did in broad daylight.

He peered into the shadows and moved forward cautiously. *Whoever it is, I'll just say I'm headed for the church house to get some wheelbarrow seed,* Chris told himself. *That had ought to shut 'em up.*

But suppose it was a Yankee soldier? A blue-uniformed Federal cavalryman might not be so eager to take Chris's sass. He stepped along, thinking he would run if it was a Yank. He didn't mean to act suspicious, skulking close to the side of the road, but he did.

"Who's there?" he asked finally. "Is that you, Lukie?"

"It's me," Lukie answered, and Chris grinned to himself. He could hear the relief in the other boy's voice. Luke had been scared too.

"Did you hear that old bobcat a-yowling a while back?" he asked Chris, coming closer. "It like to of set my teeth on edge. I can't abide to hear them varmints screeching."

Together the two boys walked down the road.

"I heared him," Chris replied. "But bobcats don't fret me none. What I dearly hate to hear is screech owls. They sound so lonesome and sorry-like."

Lukie giggled. "You mind that time we was 'coon hunting with Nate Scopes and he clumb up after the 'coon? And a big old owl got Nate by the hair of the head and wouldn't let go?"

"I reckon I won't never forget," Chris answered. "I flung my pine torch up there and I seen Nate with two big old wings flapping out on each side of his head, and I couldn't think for the life of me what had happened to him." He chuckled. "I can hear Nate yelling right now, and the owl hooting and the dogs barking. I ain't never laughed so much in my whole life."

Chris tried to step on his slanting shadow in the moonlight, hopping sideways and back. He and Lukie had had a heap of good times together. It seemed like funny things always happened when and Luke and Nate got together.

"Oh, that was funny," Lukie agreed. "But I reckon I laughed more the time my brother Bill went in the smokehouse and there was a white sheep in there after the salt. Bill, he figured it was a ghost, and he like to have come through the chinking trying to get out of there."

Chris sobered. Lukie's brother Bill was off with the Confederate troops. And just this very day Chris's brother Jethro had rushed away to join the Union army. He groaned to himself. Oh, the screech owls did right to weep and mourn across the mountaintop, for things were in a bad way here on Walden's Ridge. Chris didn't reckon folks would ever again frolic and be happy together here. Hate was like a big knife cutting folks off from each other. And it seemed like some it cut plumb in two, and the hurt was dreadful to bear.

They walked on quietly for a moment. Chris reckoned Lukie must be thinking the same kind of thoughts. Anyway it seemed like all of a sudden he remembered why they were here on Anderson Road. Luke slowed down.

"You ain't brought no rifle," he pointed out. "How you aim to shoot Yanks without no gun?"

"I never so much as mentioned shooting once," Chris answered.

"Well, you said you aimed to show me you wasn't no Yankee-lover," Luke said. "Best way to show me that is by shooting one of them blue-bellies." He patted the stock of his rifle. "That's what I brought this for," he added with a swagger.

He ain't never shot at soldiers from ambush like me and Silas, Chris thought, *or he wouldn't take on like it was so all-fired easy.* Lukie enjoyed acting important like his pa sometimes, but generally he didn't mean much by it. When it came time to act, Chris knew he could count on Luke's help.

"What I got in mind don't call for no shooting," Chris explained. "I only brought my knife."

Luke stopped then. "Well, what do you aim to do?" he asked. "I ain't going another step till I know."

Chris turned. "Come on, Lukie, don't let's stand here and talk," he pleaded. He wanted to go on and get this business over with. The longer it was put off, the more he got the fidgets. "You'll see; come on."

Luke didn't move. "I druther know."

"All right, I'll tell you," Chris said angrily. "You know the Yanks got a heap of mules penned up here on the mountain."

" 'Tain't no secret," Lukie replied. "Me and Pap went by there this morning on the way to Sawyers."

"Well, come on then," Chris said grimly. "That's where I'm headed."

"Whatever for?" Luke asked. "There's soldiers swarming around that mule pen like flies on sugar. And they got bayonets on their guns. I seen 'em. What you want to go round there for?"

Chris glared at Luke. "You said to prove I wasn't no blue-belly, didn't you? And them mules are for hauling food into Chattanooga, ain't they? If'n I let them loose, a whole heap of Yankees will starve afore the mules get rounded up again and sent to Bridgeport to fetch supplies. There! I reckon that'll prove it, won't it?"

"There was one of them soldiers had a bayonet

wide as a shovel," Luke said. "I seen it good. A bayonet like that could scoop out a man's liver and lights like a 'coon scoops a crawdad out of its shell. Pap said the soldiers don't aim to let a grasshopper get close to them mules. And they never let us stand on the road and watch 'em neither. Hollered and told us to get moving fast."

Chris was silent a minute. He hadn't really thought there'd be many soldiers at the mule pen, maybe two or three to catch the mules when needed. But then he hadn't really made any plans at all. He'd just set out headlong to let the mules loose. It had seemed simple enough then. Now he reckoned he'd have to go on and do it. He couldn't back out, no matter what Lukie said about soldiers and bayonets.

"Are you a-feared to come?" he asked Luke at last. "You was the one wanted to see me do this. You was the one wouldn't take my word I hated Yanks."

"Naw, I ain't a-feared none," Luke answered, shifting his rifle to his other hand uneasily. "But I wouldn't never be so foolish as to do something like that. A body might just as soon kiss a rattlesnake smack on the mouth as go in amongst them soldiers this night, bright as it is."

Again Chris was startled into silence. The moonlight had seemed so bright and friendly, walking along the road. He hadn't thought how plain it would show him up as he tried to undo the gate and chivy the mules out of the pen. For a minute he felt like giving up, turning clean around and trotting for home. But he set his teeth and straightened his back. He'd said he would do it, and he would. He'd outsmarted the Feds once—leastways they hadn't caught him—and he'd do it again or die trying.

"I'm a-going now," he said stubbornly. "You can come help me or not, whatever you're a mind to."

"You'd ought to be tapped for the simples," shouted Luke. And he turned and fled back down the road.

Chris started to holler "you blue-belly coward" after him, but somehow it didn't seem to matter any more. He watched the bobbing figure till it disappeared around a bend. He could go home himself now, and Lukie would never in this world know but what he'd tried and failed. He thought of those bayonets. He was scared and he knew it, but he was going through with what he'd begun.

He turned and walked swiftly on, hurrying as fast as he could, keeping close to the edge of the road and the shadows. A wind had sprung up, and that was all to the good, for on a still night you could most nigh hear a frog swallowing bugs, so quiet was the mountaintop here.

The dust kept swirling up into his eyes and nose, and by the time he got in sight of the crossroad, he had a fit of coughing. He waited in the shadows with his face in his arms, trying to smother the sound as best he could. Maybe the soldiers would think he was some new kind of night bird, or a fox with the bad quinsy.

But when he looked up, there wasn't a single soldier at the crossroads the way he'd expected. With a sigh of relief he turned off Anderson Road, following the new road cautiously. It was powerful rough and rutted. Even the moonlight wasn't much help to him, and he floundered around like a three-legged cow.

He heard the mules braying a long way off. The sound floated to him strange and thin on the wind. The breeze blew away the dust and felt cool on his chest where his shirt, damp with sweat, clung to his body. For one moment the trees bent way over, their branches lashed wildly about, and then the wind was gone. It grew dark and Chris glanced up. Little clouds were racing across the sky like so much foam-specked water. The moon bobbed about among them.

The brightness came flooding back, and Chris

pushed on down the shadowed road till he could see a fire gleaming through the trees. Persimmon shoots and pokeweed bordered the road, and he crept in among them. He didn't have to worry about being quiet with the wind so strong.

He stopped at last where he could get a good view of the fire. There wasn't a soul that Chris could see. He'd expected a heap of guards, the way Luke had talked. He could see the fence, a stake and rail fence, strong but easy to take down. He reckoned Yanks didn't know how easy it would be, for they'd built a fire in front of the gate like that was going to keep folks out, and then gone off and left it, he figured.

Or maybe they were in that hut built beside the gate. Or maybe they weren't. He wished he could see one of them. Somehow he'd rather see them than not see them. He hated the thought of those sharp bayonets creeping around behind his back. He lay there for the longest time watching the flames stream out and tower up when the wind swooped down.

At last a soldier came yawning and stretching out of the hut. He came over to the fire and put a pot on a rock beside it. He kicked at the fire, threw on some wood, and went back in the hut. A minute later he was back, dragging his gun in the dust behind him and toting an armful of truck. He sat down beside the fire and began to polish something. He held it up to inspect, and the firelight gleamed full upon it.

Chris sucked in his breath, his insides bunched up in a big knot. It was a bright, shining bayonet, wide as a shovel, just like Lukie had said.

The soldier slipped the bayonet onto his rifle. He poured something steamy from the pot into a cup and drank it. Then he buckled on his belt and shouldered his rifle. Looking at the blade gleaming up over the sentry's head, Chris flinched and ran his tongue around inside his dry mouth.

The soldier slouched off toward the far side of the stockade. Chris stood up hastily. Before the soldier reached this side, he'd better look around and make his plans.

What he didn't like was the wide space running all around the pen. There wasn't one spot where the trees and bushes grew close enough so a body could get up to the fence without being seen. In this bright moonlight it would be taking a desperate chance. A mule trumpeted out, so loud and close he near about jumped out of his skin. There were a heap of mules in the pen, so many they hardly had room to turn around. No wonder the poor critters kept shifting about restlessly, hollering out and crowding up against the fence all the time. Chris figured the beasts would welcome a hole in the fence to let them out in the woods.

A low mutter of thunder came from the south, and he glanced up to see lightning wink on and off behind a dark heap of clouds. The thunderheads rolled toward the moon. In a moment it would be black as sin here.

He grinned a little. Things were going his way for a change. Soon he could run over there and have that fence down and the mules out of the pen, and the Yanks would never see hide nor hair of him.

The lightning flickered and all the shadows swayed and reeled. Chris's heart pounded. Now he could see a figure moving in the dark.

I reckon that's the sentry, Chris told himself. *Soon as he goes by, I'll scoot for the fence*.

The sentry passed, but still Chris lay there. He couldn't make himself get up. He tried to, but his legs just wouldn't do it. He kept telling himself, *I'll just make good and sure the sentry's gone*.

He waited and waited, his eyes straining in the blackness. It was dark as God's pocket now, and he knew the soldier couldn't possibly see him, even if he was still there by the fence.

But I couldn't see him neither, thought Chris wretchedly, and that was worse. For all he knew, the sentry might be waiting right smack in front of this patch of bushes, his rifle lowered ready to jab Chris when he stood up.

The next time the lightning flashed out Chris could see there wasn't a soul near. The soldier was long gone. He took a deep breath. *Come on,* he muttered to himself. *You been waiting for this chance, ain't you?*

And at last he made it. He scampered out of the huckleberry bushes, walking fast across the clearing with his hands out before him. He reached the fence and clung to one rail. A little flurry of heavy drops spattered into the dust, and the wind made his shirt billow around him.

He began to pull at the top rail, sliding it out from between the two posts that held it. It wasn't so heavy that he couldn't handle it, but working in the dark, feeling his way along, made it hard. At last he lowered the top rail to the ground and began on the second. He had one end down and was working on the other when it slipped from his hands. It fell with a thud loud enough to wake Abraham, it seemed like.

Chris froze. He stooped there waiting for the sentry to rush up and kill him. Nothing happened, and he stood up relieved. *I reckon the wind drowned out the noise,* he thought.

He had just stepped back to the fence for another

rail when something warned him. He didn't know how he knew the guard was so close, but he did know. His heart pounded, his blood wheezed in his ears, and he did the only thing he could do—he slipped between the rails into the mule pen.

The mule nearest him snorted and stepped back. Another one suddenly loomed up behind him and blew down his neck. Chris crouched among them, trying not to frighten them, but trying too to keep from being crushed between them.

"What's the matter with you boys? What's got you so stirred up?" asked the sentry suddenly, right at Chris's elbow. "The storm don't bother you, does it?"

Trembling, Chris moved around one of the great dark shapes. If one of these critters kicked, he'd be a gone goslin. But he had to get farther away from the sentry. The soldier was bound to find those rails gone, step on those on the ground, and know something was wrong. He was bound to!

One of the mules pushed against Chris, mashing him up against another. "Great day in the morning!" Chris mumbled, and then a big hoof came down on his foot. He groaned in spite of all his efforts not to. He shoved against the mule, trying to make it shift its stand, but it stood like a rock.

Pain made Chris angry, and he hit the mule a

good clip with his fist. It moved then, startled. "Dang it, dang it, dang it," he said in a whisper. "How come is it every time I set out to do something to Yanks I end up getting worse hurt than them?" He stood on one leg and rubbed his throbbing toes.

The sentry whistled to himself.

He don't like being out here on his lonesome no more than me, Chris thought. Any moment now the soldier would find those rails gone. Or walking along, he was bound to stumble over them.

The rain was coming; Chris could hear it. The wind roared through the trees. The sentry swore. A great heavy spray of raindrops swept over and then another. In the next lightning flash, Chris could see the soldier running head down for the hut. The rain had saved him.

Chris couldn't believe it. Things *were* going his way. That was pure proper luck, and it made him feel good all over. He forgot his hurt foot and the rain stinging his face and how close he'd come to having a bayonet in him.

He pushed his way back to the fence. In a few minutes he had the other rails loose and laid on the ground. One of the mules wandered out. Chris waited. Not another beast so much as stuck its head out of the gap.

"Come along, boys," called Chris softly, though

he knew that wasn't any way to talk to mules. You had to shout and hit them.

But something had to be done. He couldn't stand here in the storm all night. Oh, he hated to go back in the pen, back among them fool critters, yet there was nothing else to do but drive them out.

He started through the gap when suddenly the whole world was on fire with lightning. A great ball of flame seemed to flash across the pen; thunder ripped down the air with a noise like a thousand cannons.

One of the mules screamed in terror and plunged toward the opening in the fence. The others pounded behind him in a wild dark mass. Dazed and half-blinded, Chris swayed in the gap. He flung up a hand and stepped backward as the great bodies came straight at him. But he hadn't a chance in this world. He didn't know which way to turn in the whirling dark.

A heavy hand seized him by the shoulder.

7

A mule bit at Chris as it ran past. The great teeth
tore a mouthful of hair from his head. The hand on
Chris's shoulder jerked him first this way, then that,
trying to dodge the mules. But then one of the beasts
slammed into them and sent them both rolling on
the ground. A big hoof flashed in front of Chris's
face, and he hollered out. Whoever had hold of Chris
pulled him aside just in time.

The ground shook beneath them as the mules
raced by. The noise was a steady roaring in his ears.
Splattering mud covered him from head to foot, and
its gritty taste was in his mouth. One mule jumped
right over him, and he didn't know for sure whether
it hit him or not. He was a heap too scared to hurt.
He reckoned he could be kicked plumb across the
mule pen and never feel it, he was so scared.

The man who had hold of Chris snatched him

suddenly to his knees. Half-dragging, half-carrying him, the man plunged through the stream of mules and staggered out against the fence. The man leaned on the rails breathing heavily, but he didn't loosen his grip for a minute.

Chris sagged wearily in his captor's grasp, wiping the mud from his face with his sleeve. The storm was slackening, though he reckoned it didn't matter now. He couldn't be any wetter. The mules scattered, and the sound of their galloping died away. That part of his plan was done with; now he had to get away. He didn't aim to be a prisoner of the Yanks, held here till the others came up and surrounded him with their bayonets. He had strength enough left to run for it, if he could just get loose.

Somebody shouted, and Chris knew the other Feds were coming. In panic he beat at the man's arm. He jerked and squirmed, but the man gripped him tighter.

"Quit that, you little fool," the man snarled in his ear. "Keep down. We've got to run for it."

Chris was so surprised he went limp all over and had to grab the fence to keep from falling. If it wasn't one of the Yanks who had him, who in blazes was it? And what did he want? And how come he wouldn't let go?

Lanterns were bobbing along beside the fence, coming closer. One soldier held up a torch that spluttered and smoked and gave off little light.

"Quick now. Get to the woods," muttered the man beside him.

Silas! Chris was almost sure it was Silas. He stumbled to his feet. But he couldn't be quick, not in this dark with the ground as rough and wet as it was.

"Yonder they go," shouted one of the soldiers.

Chris lurched along as best he could. He tripped over a stump and hit the ground hard, sliding in the mud.

The soldier with the torch suddenly threw it toward Chris. It arched up into the sky, red and fiery. Chris began to crawl. A rifle fired and then another. The bullets whirred over his head like mad hornets. The torch thudded to the ground, scattering little red sparks that sizzled as the rain put them out.

Chris was on his feet at once, running. The lanterns didn't throw much light here, but enough so that he could see the black woods ahead. At last he stumbled in among the trees and the welcome shadows. Another rifle sounded, but the shot went crashing through the bushes way down beyond Chris.

"Come on," whispered the man. "Run, afore they find us."

"Oh, I can't," moaned Chris. "I'm beat out and that's the truth."

The man grabbed him under the arms and pulled and dragged him along. It was Silas, Chris was sure now. He could feel the man's leather hunting shirt, and not a heap of folks besides Silas dressed that way. He held his hands in front of him while Silas shoved him along, but all the same he kept slapping into bushes and little trees. He'd spent so much of his time running away from Yanks lately, it looked like he'd be used to it.

Chris's legs seemed made out of iron, they were so heavy, and they wouldn't bend at all. He tried so hard to run and moved so slow, it was like a bad dream. But Silas kept on pushing him and pushing him until finally he fell in a heap and lay there in the rain.

Let Silas go on and save his skin, he thought. *Leave me for the Feds to get. I don't care any more. I done what I set out to do, and I reckon nobody can ask any more than that.*

He curled up and put his hand over his face to keep some of the dripping wet off. He lay there like a sick squirrel, heaving and gasping. It wasn't that he was so tired. He'd just been so scared for so long it seemed to take all the wind out of him. It was a while before he could get his breath properly.

The rain rattled down through the leaves, the hempines sobbed and soughed at times in the wind, but there were no more shots. No shouts of alarm rang through the woods, no soldiers came crashing through the bushes.

Silas crouched beside the boy and chuckled. "I reckon they was scared to come in the woods after us," he said. "They'll have a time trying to run them mules back inside the fence."

Chris didn't answer. The wind was cold, and he was shivering in his wet clothes. He hated the thought of the long walk home. But at least it was better than lying dead by the mule pen.

Suddenly he sat up. "Silas," he asked hoarsely. "What was you doing at the mule pen?"

"What was you doing there, Chris Brabson?" countered Silas.

"What did you think I was doing? I was letting the mules loose," answered Chris angrily.

"Well, I reckon I was there to see you did it proper," Silas said. "Come along. You got to get home. You'll get the chest fever if you stay out here in the wet much longer."

Afterwards Chris never could remember getting home. Silas must have pushed him the whole way. His legs must have moved, though they weighed so much and ached so hard. And Anderson Road must have been one great long mudhole. But he must have walked it in his sleep, so little of it came back to him.

It seemed hours later that he looked up and saw his home. It looked big and dark with its two rooms and the open dogtrot between. There wasn't any light or sign of life. The windows were shuttered against the storm.

"You better wish and pray none of your folks ain't still up," Silas muttered.

"I don't reckon they are," Chris answered. "I been out late afore this." It was true. But he'd always told his mammy where he was going before—over to Lukie's or 'coon hunting or just frolicking around on summer nights.

Chris walked down the dogtrot. A board squeaked under his feet. He fumbled at the latch string to his and Leah's room. The door behind him flew open, and he jerked around. His mammy stood there. He could see plain in the light from the fire. She was still dressed.

"Christian Brabson, wherever have you been?"

she hissed at him. "Don't you make no noise now or your pappy'll wake up and it'll be Katie-bar-the-door. You know the rest of them logs got to be brung up tomorrow. . . ."

"It's my blame, Ma'am," Silas spoke up. "I met Chris here, and we poked around in the woods till the rain catched us. It was all my doing, and we never seed a 'coon the whole time. Don't fault Chris. He wasn't the one played the fool."

"Git along with you, Silas Agee; the truth ain't in you," Mrs. Brabson said sharply.

Chris was surprised. He'd never before known his mammy to be so angry she forgot her gentle manners. She sent Silas off with a short "good night." Then she pushed Chris into his room.

"Look at you," she whispered. "Wet and muddy and shivering. Likely you got the lung fever. And you'd ought not to run around so much with that Silas. He ain't worth the powder to blow him up with."

She pulled off his wet shirt and handed him a dry one. "Now git to bed. And don't waste time about it." She eased the door to and crossed the dogtrot to her room.

Chris slipped on the dry shirt and hung his wet britches on a peg. He'd been lucky his mammy hadn't questioned him close about where he and Silas had been. He was glad Silas had been there to speak up and say what he did. It wasn't exactly lying, though it wasn't the truth. It made him uneasy, for he wasn't used to deceiving. It never got a body anything but trouble.

He crawled into bed, rattling the corn shucks. Leah turned in her bed but didn't wake. He pulled up all the coverlids he found. He was icy cold all over. Stretching out, his toes touched the hot stone, wrapped in a cloth, at the foot of his bed.

He grinned a little to himself. Wasn't that just like his mammy—to scold and fuss like that and all the time planning for his comfort?

He lay there with the warmth creeping slowly up his legs. He thought about what he had done tonight. He reckoned Lukie would know now he wasn't a blue-belly. But what about Silas? Silas, who'd been around so handy to save his life. What was Silas doing there?

Was Silas a spy? Was that how come he was always so knowing about what went on in the valley? Was that how come he took squirrels down to trade to the Yanks, hoping to see or hear something he could report back to the Confederates?

Chris tried to think, tried to remember things Silas had said that might give him away. But he was powerful tired. He couldn't get things straight in his mind, to save him. Warmth from the stone stole over his whole body. The shuck mattress was soft as lambs' wool.

He was asleep.

8

Chris got up the next morning, heavy-eyed and weary. His mammy gave him a look when he sat down to eat, but nobody said anything to him. Nobody asked where he'd been, nobody wanted to know how come his arms were all brier-scratched, or how come he favored one foot when he walked.

Nobody accused him of turning the Yankee mules loose neither, but then his folks hadn't heard about it yet. He sure hoped when they did, they wouldn't figure it was him. He flinched at having to tell his pa he'd spent the night dodging Yankee bullets in a rainstorm.

A body would think he'd be proud and head high this morning. He'd done a good job for General Lee, and he'd helped out General Bragg at the risk of his neck. But it was queer. He just felt dull and tired, and somehow he couldn't look his mammy square in the eye. He ate his buttermilk and lye hominy without raising his eyes from his bowl.

"Make haste, Chris; there's work to be done," Mr. Brabson called from the door.

"Yes, sir," Chris answered. He knew it well enough. He hoped General Braxton Bragg knew how much it cost him to get out and snake up logs on this day of all days. He didn't know how he'd hold out.

And then it turned out he didn't have to. First off, one of the chains broke. Then his mammy wanted the loom set up, and his father had to quit to help her. Chris chopped a few logs and fetched a piece of cedar for his pappy to whittle a shuttle out of. And the morning passed away without him doing a lick of hard work.

After dinner Mrs. Brabson set Chris and Leah to work hunting eggs. The hens were bad about laying out in the bushes.

"Darn these old hens," moaned Leah. "I'll get dew poisoning wading around in these here wet weeds."

The high grass was still damp from last night's rain. The sky was overcast and the day was cool.

"Well, go on home then," said Chris. "I'll look by myself." He was searching along the fence-row when suddenly he heard a dog barking. He looked up and saw Jethro's old hound Thumb running along the edge of the clearing, and behind him came Sallie Jean and the baby, Liddy.

Chris didn't go to meet them. Sallie Jean was a mighty pretty young woman and a heap of good company, but he couldn't forget her husband had gone to be a Federal soldier, to wear a hateful blue uniform like the rest of the blue-bellies.

"Mammy," called Leah. "Here comes Sallie Jean."

Mrs. Brabson came running out of the house.

"I come over to bring you a little something," said Sallie Jean. She held out a poke. "I knowed you was in need of meal. Since Jethro left, there's a heap more at our house than me and Liddy can use, so I brung you some."

"Oh, we wasn't in need," cried Mrs. Brabson. "We was making out all right, Sallie Jean. You'd ought to keep it. You ain't got menfolks to hunt for you, the way we have."

"It's yours, by rights," Sallie Jean went on. "You give us the seed corn. And me and Jethro ain't forgot how much help we got with the clearing and the plowing last spring."

Chris wanted his mammy to take that meal and

quit being so mannerly. The Yanks had taken the Brabsons' meal. Brabsons might as well take a little of it back.

"Well," agreed Mrs. Brabson, "you stay for supper, Sallie Jean, and help us eat it."

"Oh, I will. And I can't thank ye enough," replied Sallie Jean fervently. "I declare it's lonesome there in the cabin with Jethro gone. And it's such a gray, gloomy old day. I kept telling myself all morning it ain't no way for a soldier's wife to act, but I just couldn't hardly stand it, and that's a fact. I come over to bring the meal, but I come for company, too."

"Well, set down and make yourself to home," Mrs. Brabson told her. "You're welcome as water. You stay as long as you like. We was kind of honing for a friendly face ourselves. Now I'm proud you come. Me and Leah got all these nuts to crack, and you can help us do it."

She turned and called, "Alex, Sallie Jean's here." She looked around. "And yonder's Chris. Bring the eggs, Chris, and speak to Sallie Jean."

Mr. Brabson came out of the cabin. He squatted down and held out his arms. The baby walked to him, and Mr. Brabson looked mighty pleased. "I knowed when that chain broke it was a sign for me to quit work and take the day off." He grinned. "We'll just all get us a setting-down task and make a play-party out of this here afternoon."

And that was another thing he could thank Sallie Jean for, Chris thought, as he walked toward the cabin. He wouldn't have to work much the rest of the day. But he wished it was some Rebel girl who'd brought him such good fortune. Anyway, he didn't aim to have anything to do with her, or Liddy either.

He nodded to Sallie Jean and carried the eggs into the house. He stayed in a long time, not doing anything, just sitting on his mammy's big bedstead thinking about Silas. Was Silas really a spy?

When he came out, they were all sitting in the dogtrot, the womenfolks cracking nuts and his pappy working on the shuttle.

"Get that whetstone, Chris, and put a good edge on them two axes there," Mr. Brabson said. "They're too dull to chop thin mud."

Chris silently fetched the whetstone and the axes and set to work.

"Oh, here's a big old worm in this here walnut," cried Sallie Jean. "You want me to save him for you, Leah?"

"Save him for Chris," answered Leah. "Worms is what he likes best to eat."

"Well, it must be good for him," said Sallie Jean, laughing. "He looks most nigh as big as Jethro right now."

Chris tested the edge of the blade with his thumb. He wasn't going to laugh and take on over Leah's foolishness. He wasn't even going to talk to Sallie Jean. And here came Liddy, waddling over to where he sat. He wasn't going to notice her, though he reckoned she was the prettiest baby in the wide world.

Liddy stopped right beside Chris. She squatted down and watched him, solemn as a baby owl. Her blue eyes were wide and knowing, her hair goldy-red and curly. When she looked up at Chris suddenly, he dropped his ax and reached down and hugged her small round body against him.

"Don't be no Yank, Liddy," he whispered into her pink ear. "Don't ever be no Yank."

Liddy patted his hand. "Baby," she said. It was the only word she knew.

The afternoon wore on. Chris didn't mean to join in the fun. But such a heap of funny tales got told and Sallie Jean had such a catching giggle, he forgot. He laughed with the rest of them, and once in a while he managed to slip a word in edgewise between Leah's chatter and his mammy's stories.

Suddenly Sallie Jean jumped up. "Oh, my soul,

it's a-gitting dark. I can't stay to eat. It'll be long past candlelight afore I get home."

"Oh, now, Sallie Jean," Mrs. Brabson reproved her. "You know you ain't going home this night. We aimed for you to stay two, three days, visit us good."

"Well," said Sallie Jean slowly, "I don't really hanker to go home. I reckon I might as well stay this night anyway. I shut up my hens afore I left home, and my cow's dry. I ain't really got nothing to go home for."

For a minute she looked sad, as though she might cry.

"We'll get supper started right now," Mrs. Brabson said. "Come along, we'll have us a feast."

The supper meal was good. Chris could hardly get enough of the crisp corn bread. His mammy fetched out some honey and fried the last of the side meat, and they had eggs and buttermilk.

"And these here little cabbages that come along so late, they like to got burned up in the drought," said Mrs. Brabson. "They taste good, now, don't they? And I would have left them out there for the frost, only they're all we got now."

When the meal was over, Sallie Jean and Mrs. Brabson cleaned up the dishes. It was dark outside and the door was shut. For the first time this fall the night air was cool and crisp. Chris brought in a load of wood, then he went across the dogtrot for a poke of beechnuts. Sallie Jean and the children sat on the floor between the Brabsons. It was quiet for a moment in the fire-lit room.

"My ring!" cried Leah, remembering. "Let me show Sallie Jean my ring." She ran to get it. "Ain't it grand?" she asked. "I aim to get me a hoop skirt, and then I'll be a lady for fair."

"Oh, it's a fine pretty ring," Sallie Jean answered, catching hold of Leah's hand. "And you know what I heared? I heared Betsy Poteet had a hoop skirt. She went down to Chattanooga and did a heap of weaving for a fine lady. And she took the hoop skirt for payment. Wouldn't have meal or meat or even salt, scarce as it is. She come home, and her mammy was so mad she hit Betsy a lick with a piece of firewood, for the Poteets had counted on meal as payment. But Betsy said it was worth it; she'd always craved a hoop skirt above all things."

"One good thing, we don't have to hire somebody to do our spinning and weaving for us," Mrs. Brabson commented. "I reckon there ain't many folks here on Walden's Ridge that has forgot how to do those things. Us Brabsons has always worn homespun and always will, I reckon."

"Oh, Mammy," wailed Leah. "Can't I even have a store-boughten dress to git married in?"

"Great day in the morning!" exclaimed Mr. Brabson. "I hope you ain't planning on getting married any day right soon."

"Who all told you that about Betsy?" asked Mrs. Brabson.

"Hattie Allen told me. She come by to give me some red root to dye a dress with," explained Sallie Jean. "It was mighty thoughty of her."

"Oh, she's a kind-hearted girl, like her mammy," Mrs. Brabson said. "Her mammy and me was friends when we was young, up to the time she got married. Her name was Zilpah Ware then, and she was lively, always up to something. I reckon I've told the story about the time her and me had a dumb supper."

"A dumb supper!" cried Leah. "Whatever's that?"

Chris almost told her it was a meal for stupid little girls, but he didn't want to start an argument.

"Well, I reckon I ain't told this tale afore," said Mrs. Brabson, "because there ain't no point to it if a body don't know what a dumb supper is. Leah, it used to be girls were always having dumb suppers. That was the only sure way to tell who they was going to marry."

"I know about it," Sallie Jean said. "At a dumb supper you can't talk and you walk backward making the corn bread and setting the table."

"That's right." Mrs. Brabson nodded. "You do

everything in silence. You're supposed to do it late at night, and at midnight you see your future husband. Well, me and Zilpah got the bread made in plenty of time and put a piece on each of the four plates."

"Four plates for just the two of you?" asked Chris.

"Yes, there was a plate for each of us and, beside us, a plate for our future husbands to set," explained Mrs. Brabson. "You see, this ghost is supposed to come in at midnight and set down beside you and eat the corn bread."

"Ghost!" Leah's eyes popped wide open. She was scared to death of "ha'nts."

"Ghost or spirit or something," Sallie Jean put in. "And if a girl can see who it is, she'll know her husband. But if she can't make out the dark figure, she'll die within a year of a dire disease."

Leah gasped.

"At first me and Zilpah was hard put not to laugh," Mrs. Brabson went on. "We was just doing this for foolishness. But we sat at the table and never said a word, just held in the giggles. The candle burned between us. And when it was getting near twelve o'clock, we opened the door and blew out the candle. We sat there in the dark waiting. It was powerful quiet all of a sudden. And I began to get sort of uneasy. I'd never in my life seen a ghost, but I had goose prickles all over me. The fire had died down after we cooked the bread, for it was a warmish night. I've never known a cabin so dark. Then it was midnight, and all of a sudden we heard footsteps—running steps—and they were headed straight for the cabin. Zilpah kind of moaned, but I was too scared to make a sound. I could feel the hair raise up all over my scalp."

Chris felt a tingling along his neck. Leah gulped and glanced over her shoulder into the shadows at the back of the room.

"The steps come closer and closer, and then they was in the room. Suddenly there was a dark shape standing right beside me. I was scared tee-total, I tell you. And it began fumbling at the table, clinking the spoons together. And a voice said, Zilpah! kind of low and scary-like. Zilpah let out a shriek you could hear to the ocean, and I was ready to run, only that thing was between me and the door."

"Oh, Mammy," cried Leah, putting her hand over her eyes. "Hurry and tell what it was."

"Well, finally I had the sense to grab a candle and shove it down in the hot ashes and blow up a spark. When the wick caught, I stood up and turned around, and there stood a man wild-eyed and bloody and white as a ghost, a man I hadn't never laid eyes on before. He was standing right in the place Zilpah had set for her husband's ghost. And he said, 'What in the world sort of foolishment are you two up to? You like to have scared the gizzard out of me!'

"You see, it was Sam Allen. And he and Zilpah's brother had been out hunting. Zilpah's brother fell and cut his leg, and Sam had run to get some cobwebs and soot to staunch the blood. He was sure provoked with us two sillies."

"Did he eat the corn bread?" asked Leah, taking her hand down at last.

"Never did, but him and Zilpah got hitched anyhow," answered Mammy.

Sallie Jean gave a little shiver. "Now ain't that a scary tale?" she asked. "It puts me in mind of one I heard when I was little that always scared me. It was about a pretty girl and a man who come from a far-off place to court her. And one day he said to her, 'Meet me tonight by the big oak tree at moonrise, and we'll run off and get married.' She said she would, 'cause she loved him so. When she got to the oak that night, the moon wasn't up and her lover wasn't there. She waited in the dark till she heared two men a-coming. She got scared and climbed up in the tree. The men stopped right under her and began to dig a hole. She heared how they planned to kill some girl for her money and silver spoons and bury her in that hole. She listened and shivered and hoped her lover wouldn't come by. Then the moon rose, and she saw that one of the men was her lover. Oh, it made her blood turn cold, but she didn't cry out. She waited in the tree till they had gone and climbed down and ran home. Next day her suitor came riding by and asked where she was the night before. And she answered:

> 'Riddledee, riddledee, riddledee right,
> Guess where I sat a long time last night,
> Up in the boughs my heart did ache
> To see the hole the fox did make.'

And then her suitor knew. So he left out of there in a hurry, and he ain't been seen since."

Chris reckoned that girl in the tree must have felt a little bit the way he did when he was hanging on the cliff and the Yanks were after him. Oh, they'd both had narrow escapes.

"That's a little like what we used to call a neck riddle," said Mr. Brabson.

"Whatever's that?" asked Sallie Jean.

"Why, it's where a man's got to be hung for some crime or other, and they offer to let him go free can he make up a riddle nobody can guess.

And he always does and saves his neck," Mr. Brabson explained. "Or, maybe we just don't hear about the ones that couldn't make up a good enough riddle."

"Now here's a dandy riddle," exclaimed Mrs. Brabson. "What's higher without a head than with a head?"

They all thought for a moment. Leah wrung her hands and bounced up and down. "Don't let Chris guess till I do," she cried. "He always answers, and I never git to guess."

"Well, what's your guess?" asked Mr. Brabson, getting a handful of beechnuts.

"I give up," said Leah finally.

"That's a good guess," said Chris scornfully. "Now I guess a hog. When it's been slaughtered and tied up to the rafters, it's a heap taller than before its head was cut off."

Mrs. Brabson smiled but shook her head. "The answer is a pillow," she said.

"But a pillow ain't got no head," pointed out Leah.

"And that's when it's fluffed up higher, stupid," Chris told her, poking her in the ribs. She turned and slapped his hand, then moved over to the hearth to sit before he could slap her back.

Liddy, sleeping on the big bed, woke up and began to cry. Leah jumped up and ran to her. She began to pat the baby, talking to her soothingly. But Liddy went on wailing.

"Here, I'll sing to her," said Sallie Jean, getting up. "She won't hardly go back to sleep without I sing to her."

She took up the baby and sat down by the fire, swaying back and forth. She began to sing softly:

"The sow took the measles and died in the spring.
 And what do ye think I made of her hide?
 The very best saddle ye ever did ride.
 Saddle or bridle or any such thing,
 The sow took the measles and died in the spring."

Chris stared sleepily into the fire. He was warm and full of good food and almost lighthearted. It was easy to forget about war and the way Yanks had come raiding across the land and all the other troubles, sitting here listening to Sallie Jean. This was the way folks used to be all the time, gay and friendly and gentle-hearted. It was enough to crack your heart in two to think how times had changed.

"Jennifer, Jenny and Rosemary," sang Sallie Jean.

Chris yawned. He'd have to go to bed before he fell asleep here on the floor. He stood up quietly and went to the door. He pulled up the latch and stepped halfway out, ready to cross the dogtrot.

Out across the yard he could see a fire at one corner of the shed and a dark figure squatting there, fanning the flames.

"Pappy!" cried out Chris. "Somebody's a-setting fire to the shed."

Mr. Brabson sprang up so fast his chair turned over. It clattered to the floor, and Liddy woke again and began to wail.

"What's afire, Alex?" called Mrs. Brabson.

Mr. Brabson peered over Chris's shoulder. "Dang!" he muttered.

"That 'un started it, there under the hickory," Chris pointed, flinging the door open wider. "I can see good enough to shoot him. Let me fetch my rifle." He started across the dogtrot.

Mr. Brabson seized him roughly by the shoulder. "There'll be no shooting," he declared firmly. He pulled Chris back. "Shooting is the start of no end of troubles. We'll stay inside out of the way. There ain't no point in tangling with them hotheads out there."

Chris's mouth hung open. His pappy must be addled just to stand idly by while somebody burned down the farm.

"Is the shed a-burning?" asked Mrs. Brabson. "Who in the world would do such a thing? Alex, ain't you going to stop them? Why would anybody want to burn our shed?"

Leah came wiggling between her father and Chris. "Let me see the fire," she begged. "Let me see, Pappy!"

Mr. Brabson let go of Chris and grabbed Leah. "Don't you set foot out there," he growled. "Ain't you heared me? Them fellers is up to no good, and it would behoove us to lay low. Shut that door, Chris!"

"But who is it?" asked Mrs. Brabson again, rubbing her hands together nervously. "Who's out there?"

Chris took one last look at the fire. The shed was old; its logs and shingles were half-rotten and dry. It burned like punk wood, flaring up in long streamers of sparks toward the sky. Among the trees shadows wavered back and forth. Who was out there? Who had done a mean thing like this to the Brabsons?

He shut the door. They could still hear the fire crackling and popping and the whoops and yells from the men watching.

He turned back into the room. There stood Sallie Jean, white-faced and big-eyed, with Liddy in her arms. At the sight of her Chris knew. Her face told him plain as could be it was because of Jethro the shed had been set on fire. Those were Confederate sympathizers out there hollering around the burning logs like a bunch of drunk Indians.

It came over him in a hot rush then that nobody stopped to think Chris Brabson wasn't a Yankee lover. Didn't those men out there know how he'd risked his neck to set the mules loose? Didn't they know he hated Yanks, had fired on the cavalry and most nigh got dropped over a cliff for his pains?

But no. He got put in the same class with the rest of the Brabsons, folks who had turned against their friends and neighbors and joined up with the blue-bellies. And all on account of Jethro.

He clenched his fists. It wasn't right. He didn't know anything else he could do to prove he hated the Yanks. And nobody paid him any mind.

Sallie Jean rocked the baby back and forth. Finally she said in a strained voice, "You reckon they been out to my cabin first?"

"Likely not," Mr. Brabson reassured her. "It's too far. But I'm glad you was here with us and not out there by yourself. You'd best make up your mind to come stay with us for a spell. We'll go over to-morrow and git your truck and bring it here."

Mrs. Brabson looked from Sallie Jean to her husband. "You mean it was on account of Jethro, then, somebody done us this meanness?" she cried. Her shoulders drooped, and she put her hand up to her eyes. "They'd ought to pay. They'd ought to go to jail. If a body can't follow his conscience and do what he thinks is right, what is the world coming to?"

"These be wartimes, Betsy," Mr. Brabson answered his wife wearily. "Folks don't act in natural ways during wartimes, it seems like."

Sallie Jean went up to Mrs. Brabson. "Oh, I'm sorry as I can be," she said. "It's sorry times, the Lord knows it is, but it looks like me and Jethro's made it harder for you folks than ever."

Mrs. Brabson looked down at Liddy, drowsing on her mother's shoulder. Suddenly she straightened up and took the baby from Sallie Jean. "Now don't talk like that," she said briskly. "There's always some folks mean enough to do anything. Jethro's our son, and we brought him up to do what he figured was the right thing to do. It ain't nobody's blame and surely it ain't yours."

"It don't matter a heap about the shed anyway," spoke up Mr. Brabson. "It was half-doty already, and there wasn't a power of things in it. The axes was in the dogtrot."

Oh, not a power of things, Chris thought bitterly. Just the harness that they couldn't use because the Yanks had taken the horse, and the hoes they couldn't use because the Yanks had taken the seed corn and potatoes, and the iron anvil his great-great-grandpappy had brought from Pennsylvania that they never used anyway.

"Wonder how come Thumb didn't bark?" asked Sallie Jean. "I hope nothing ain't happened to him. Jethro thinks the world of that dog."

"Oh, likely he's gone off in the woods a-hunting something," Mr. Brabson answered. "It wouldn't have helped us none if'n he had been here to bark."

No, it wouldn't have helped. Barking dogs or letting mules loose or getting robbed by Yankee soldiers—nothing helped. Folks were going to hate the Brabsons no matter what. "If'n I had a rope, I'd hang myself," Chris muttered. "Or some blue-belly. Or something."

"They ain't making any noise out there now," Mrs. Brabson remarked.

Mr. Brabson stood at the door listening. "As soon as we're sure they're gone, we'd best get to bed."

Suddenly, close to the house, right up in the

dogtrot it seemed to Chris, somebody yelled out. "This here's what happens to Yankee-lovers," the man bawled. "Next time, it'll be the house."

Chris ran to the window and threw open the shutter. He wanted a glimpse of this man, so later he could tell him the truth, tell him that Chris Brabson was no Yankee-lover but a true and loyal Tennessean who would never turn against his own kind.

There was nobody near the house that he could see. The shed was mostly embers now, but one piece of log still burned bright enough for him to make out Lukie Trantham's pap moving off across the edge of the clearing. And Hoke Edwin and over there— Chris could hardly believe his eyes! He leaned out the window to see better, and it was true. He could see the third man plainest of all, a man with a beard and a long hunting shirt. Silas Agee!

10

It was a restless night. Liddy kept wailing, and Leah had a nightmare and woke up crying. Chris himself, tired as he was, lay awake the longest, sore-hearted and troubled. He had thought Silas was his friend. But Silas had come along to burn the shed and never lifted a hand to stop the others, never said, "There's a boy in the house that's a true Southern boy, who's done a heap to make up for his brother going off to the Union army."

Maybe the other men didn't know what Chris had done. But Silas knew, knew better than anyone but Chris himself. Why hadn't he spoken out in Chris's favor?

It wasn't so much the loss of the shed. It was the blow to Chris's pride, to have his deeds and feelings ignored. And now everybody for miles around would know the Brabsons—all the Brabsons—had been brought low, had been shamed and humbled.

Next morning Chris slept late. When he woke up, Sallie Jean was leaving. He listened to the talk outside as he dressed.

"Yonder comes Thumb now to take me home," she cried. "Where was you last night, you worthless varmint?"

"You take him inside and keep him there tonight," instructed Mrs. Brabson. "We surely wish you would stay a while longer."

"No, I aim to stay at my place," Sallie Jean answered. "There's a heap to do. I'll keep busy. And I'll be back soon and stay two, three days."

Sallie Jean was gone, but Chris had a heap more to think about than his married kin. He had to decide what he'd do about Silas. He reckoned they were no longer friends, the way Silas had acted last night. It was a thing hard to believe.

Maybe it wasn't Silas, Chris told himself. *Likely Silas was nowheres near this house last night.*

He tried hard to believe that as he helped his pappy go through the ashes of the shed. But he'd seen Silas plain, clear as light. The only thing for him to do, Chris decided, was to forget about it. He and Mr. Brabson found the hoe blades and the chains and bits of metal still worth saving for some possible use some day.

"These things ain't hardly harmed," said Mr.

Brabson. "The shed went up so quick, the fire didn't rightly have time to get good and hot. But it'll take a spell to get some more harness fixed up for us two mules to snake logs with. Tell you what, Chris, you do some chopping whilst I see can I find any leather in the loft. It'll make your mammy feel better if'n we got a few back logs ready."

Chris set to work. His arms swung up and down in an easy rhythm. The sound of the ax thwacking into the solid wood seemed to soothe him and keep his mind off his troubles.

"A willing worker is a delight to the Lord," said Mr. Brabson when he came to see what Chris had done. "That's a good morning's work, Chris. You've earned your vittles this day. Come eat."

But after the noonday meal, things didn't go so well. Chris couldn't keep a good edge on his ax blade. One of the trees had a cross-grained scar that was as hard as stone to chop through. He had to rest often, and he went back to thinking about Silas and the queer way he'd acted.

Seems like Silas was the onliest friend I had, he told himself sadly. *And now I ain't even got him.*

It plagued him the whole afternoon, ate at him like a canker does wood, till he could stand it no longer. He dropped his ax and straightened his back.

"There ain't no use worrying over it any more," he said aloud. "I'll just go over to Silas right now and ask him plain. I'll say, 'Silas, how come you to burn our shed down last night?'"

He walked to the spring and took a long drink. He rubbed the cool water over his face and neck, and then he set out. There was a good chance Silas wouldn't be home. It was always hard to lay a finger on Silas. He was here, there, and gone.

If'n he ain't home, I'll wait for him, thought Chris grimly. *This here has worried me long enough.*

There was an old iron mine, long since abandoned, close to Silas's cabin. Water had seeped into it and filled it till it was a deep brown pool. Chris stood staring down into the dark water. What was he going to do if Silas admitted he had burned the shed? It made Chris uneasy, and he had halfway a mind to turn back home and never let on he'd seen anybody last night.

He got to thinking how Silas jumped in this pond water once or twice a year and took a bath. He said the iron in the water strengthened his body. Silas was like that. He had a reason for doing things most always, and if Chris asked him, Silas would tell why he took part in the burning. He threw a flat rock into the pool and went on.

Silas was home. Chris could see smoke rising from the rickety cat-and-stick chimney. And he could smell meat cooking.

The cabin was a tumble-down affair. Half the chinking was gone from between the logs, and an old deer hide covered a hole in the roof. But Silas didn't seem to care. He seemed happy as most folks. Happier than some, Chris thought.

The door was open, and he knocked on the door frame. Silas looked around from where he squatted on the hearth. Meat was spitted over the fire, and the juice sizzled in the ashes.

"Well, Chris, come on in, come on in," cried Silas. "You're just in time to help me eat this here 'possum." He winked at the boy.

Chris could see very well it was a half a shoat. Most folks knew Silas helped himself every now and then to pigs running loose in the woods. It was the way he was, and folks had got used to putting up with him.

"Just let it brown the least more and I'll cut you off a tasty piece," Silas went on. "It won't be long now. Sit down, boy."

Chris shook his head. "Silas," he said gruffly. "Some folks burned down our shed last night."

Silas cut his eyes around at Chris. "For a fact," he exclaimed.

Chris set his mouth stubbornly. He'd gone so far, and he didn't aim to back down. "I got me a good look at some of them," he said. "And one was you."

Silas stood up and seized the boy's arm. "Your pappy didn't see me, did he?" he asked.

Chris shook off the man's hand. "Nobody seen you but me," he said coldly. "And I wished I hadn't. Why did you do it, Silas? I'd of reckoned a true friend would of spoke up and said I was a real Southern boy and not let them others burn down my shed."

Silas bent down and turned the meat over. "I reckon you got a right to be put out," he said. "I was there all right. Them fellers was truly roused up about Jethro and out to do any sort of meanness. I reckon if I hadn't been along"—he stood up and faced Chris—"if I hadn't been along, they'd of done worse. I couldn't keep them from burning the shed, but I was handy to keep you folks from harm."

Chris stood there a minute, thinking over Silas's words in his head. If it was true, then Silas had done the Brabsons a favor.

"I'm obliged to you," he said at last. "But how come you didn't tell them about me? I reckon they wouldn't of harmed us if they had knowed it was me turned the mules loose and all that. You could have told them and they'd of left us alone."

"Oh, in the mood they was in, they wouldn't never in this wide world have believed me," Silas told him, poking at the fire. "Why, I don't hardly credit it myself, a young boy doing a dangerous thing like that. They would of thought I was making it up to try to save you folks. It might have aggravated them even more than they was already. Especially since the Yankees give out it was the lightning scared the mules and made them knock down the fence."

He looked out the doorway a minute. "Don't you worry none," he said, turning back. "The truth will out. They'll learn it was you done it soon enough. But it wouldn't do for the news to come from me right at that very moment, do you see?"

"But you was there at the mule pen!" cried Chris. "You seen it all. How come you think they wouldn't believe you?"

Silas stuck a knife into the meat. " 'Cause maybe I didn't want them to know I was there," he said briefly. " 'Cause maybe I had my reasons."

Chris was silent. What had Silas been doing at the mule pen? What had Silas been doing all those times he went into Chattanooga? How come Silas to know so much other folks didn't know?

"Silas," he said sharply. "Be you a spy?"

Silas dropped his knife. "A body can git hanged for spying," he answered. "It ain't a fit subject for idle talk. I'd be mighty careful afore I'd ask a man that, Chris."

"I never said you was," Chris pointed out.

"No," said Silas. "You didn't. And I didn't say I was neither. That ain't to say I don't keep my eyes and ears open, same as any good Southerner would. And if'n"—he looked at Chris slyly—"I say if'n . . . if'n I was to see or hear anything worthwhile, I reckon there'd be ways to get it to the folks it would do the most good."

Chris's heart thumped. Silas must be a spy. He hadn't come right out and said he wasn't. He *must* be.

"Now, you, Chris," Silas jabbed with his knife at the boy, "you'd be a fine one to spy. Your brother's in the Union army, your shed's been burned, folks all think you're a Yank sympathizer. You might hear most anything from folks that favor the North. They'd speak out in front of you where they wouldn't in front of me, for instance."

He cut a piece of the pork and laid it on a wood chip and handed it to the boy. Chris took it, keeping his eyes on Silas. Was the hunter trying to tell him he could help? Could he truly be a spy for the Confederate army?

"You might almost say it would be a good thing the Brabsons' shed got burned," Silas went on. "Now everybody knows for sure the Brabsons are blue-bellies—all the Brabsons, including Chris. It most looks like it had been planned that way, don't it?"

A tremor ran through Chris. Silas had meant all along for Chris to help him. He'd plotted it all so folks would think Chris was a Yankee-lover, so he could help with the spying.

Silas cut a piece from the roast for himself. "Of course it'd look that way was I a real spy and able to tote messages to General Bragg," he said lightly. "Eat up, Chris, there's aplenty more 'possum."

Chris sat down then. He cut a piece of his meat and slowly, thoughtfully, he chewed it.

11

Chris flung the two squirrels and the scrawny raccoon down on the ground. "That ain't what you might call slathers of game," he said aloud in disgust. "Mammy ain't going to be pleased one whit with so little."

He couldn't help it. He'd welcomed this chance to do a day's hunting. Leaving all his tasks, he'd gone out in the woods this morning lighthearted and cocksure. There wasn't a doubt in his mind but what he'd shoot a deer or a fat old bear for his family. But he hadn't.

He leaned his gun against a tree and stretched his arms over his head. He was as full of kinks as a rifle spring. And he hated having so little to show for a day's work. It seemed like everything he set his hand to lately went wrong. The Brabsons were bad off for meat, and he'd tramped the mountaintop far and wide, yet these three varmints were all he'd seen. Where had all the beasts got to? It couldn't have been far from here that he and Silas had seen a deer the day they had ambushed the cavalry.

He glanced around, frowning to think about that bad day. But it was on this very spot, near as he could remember, that he'd started to leave the path and climb a tree to hide. Oh, it seemed like forever and a day ago instead of just last Saturday.

Picking up his gun and the game, he walked on through the trees and out onto the great flat top of the bluff. Over there was the crack where he had hung by his fingertips. He turned away quickly. It still gave him a weak feeling in his stomach to think about those jagged rocks and him dangling over them.

And right about here the two Yanks had sat on their horses and talked. He wished two would come along right now. Though it killed him, he would bow and scrape like he thought the world and all of blue-bellies. Oh, he'd talk to them, friendly as a pup, and they wouldn't think for one minute he was a Rebel boy taking in every word they were saying. They would begin to tell him how the Federal army was leaving Chattanooga and fortifying Walden's Ridge. And quick as he could, he'd get the information to Silas.

He grinned to himself, thinking how easy it would be to slip through the bushes. Nobody would see Chris Brabson go to Silas's, nobody would suspect a thing till the big battle was over and the Rebels were victorious. Then everybody would wonder how come the Rebels to know where to attack and when. And General Bragg would say, "Why, Chris Brabson done all my spying. Ask him!"

Folks would come to see General Bragg thank Chris and praise him for his daring and cleverness. Likely the General would beg Chris to join his army to show the Rebel soldiers how to shoot, to teach the other spies all his tricks. And his mammy would beg him not to go. The General would say that Chris Brabson was needed to drive the Yankees plumb out of Tennessee. And Chris would ride off to war with everybody cheering. He wouldn't go sneaking off like Jethro did, hardly more than telling he was going before he was gone. No sirree, he'd leave likely with a band playing.

What was the matter with him? He was acting like Leah, making up tales this way.

I ain't got the least chance to do any spying, he thought. *There's mighty little would happen on Walden's Ridge. And I'd be snaking logs when it did happen and not know about it till too late.*

It was the living truth. No matter how much he might want to help, there wasn't anything he could do. He couldn't run wild day and night the way Silas did.

The whole of Sequatchie Valley lay stretched out below him, yellow and brown and green. Chris wished he had some reason to go to the valley. A body could do a heap of spying down there. Howsomever, he wouldn't want to live there. It couldn't be so fine as the mountaintop.

He turned to leave. But something he'd seen nagged at him a little. What was that he'd seen moving? He whipped back around and moved closer to the edge of the bluff. Great day in the morning! Wagons! Hundreds and hundreds of them! As far as he could see, they stretched along the road, one after another. It looked like all the wagons in the world headed straight for Walden's Ridge.

Only a few turned at Anderson's Crossroads and took the road up the mountain. The rest waited on the road back toward Jasper. What were they doing? He watched carefully. Why, they were going to make camp for the night. A few wagons were pulling into a field.

A troop of cavalry jogged in and out among the mules and wagons. They looked like a mighty puny handful of soldiers to take care of such a great supply train. You might think they'd have soldiers aplenty to guard.

It was too bad the Confederates weren't handy. It wouldn't take a heap of sharp-shooting Rebels to get shut of those blue-coats and take those wagons and whatever was in them. He wished General Bragg knew about this.

And suddenly Chris turned and began to run. He was a woodenhead, for a fact, standing there watching when he ought to be getting the news to Silas as fast as his legs could tote him. Silas would know what to do. Silas could get the information to the Southern army if anybody could. This was the very thing spies were for!

When he finally got back home, his legs were shaking with weariness. It was a long run—all the way to Silas's and then back to the Brabson clearing. He sank down on a log and sat there for a minute, panting and letting his whole body go limp. By and by he sat up and took out his knife and began to skin the squirrels.

Leah, coming up from the spring, saw him. She set her piggin of water down with a thump and came over to him, her hands on her hips.

"Is that all you got?" she asked. "Mammy'll be mad."

Chris said nothing.

"I reckon she's mad already," Leah went on. "You been gone so long. I had to fetch in the wood and water all by myself."

"Is that a fact?" asked Chris mildly.

"Yes, and Pappy's mad on account of you was gone so long he had to go over to Sallie Jean's hisself," stated Leah, twisting so her pigtails would swing back and forth. "He wanted to borrow Jethro's harness."

Chris groaned a little. That was a long walk over there. He'd more than halfway promised his father he'd get back from hunting in time to go.

"I reckon you'll git a good licking when he gets home," Leah said hopefully.

"I reckon you'll git one if you don't tote that water in mighty quick," Chris retorted.

Leah stuck out her tongue at him, but she walked back to her piggin. "Yonder comes Pappy now," she called. "You'd better run, for I reckon he's got a hickory in his hand."

Chris didn't even look up. He wouldn't give Leah that much satisfaction. He'd know soon enough if his pappy was coming. He finished the squirrels and began on the 'coon.

Well, he might not be much of a hunter, but he was a good spy. Silas had said so. Chris had hardly told his news before Silas had on his hat and was ready to leave to tell the Confederates to come hurrying.

Chris heard footsteps. It was Pappy, for a fact. Still he didn't look up. He didn't think he'd get a licking for being late. But if he did, it wouldn't be the first one. Nor the last, he reckoned.

"Come on inside, Chris," Mr. Brabson called as he crossed the clearing and stepped up on the dogtrot. "I got a heap of news to tell."

Chris looked up then, a little startled. Had the Confederates already got to the wagon train? No, he knew they couldn't have.

"Yes, sir, I'm a-coming," Chris answered. But he took time to finish skinning the 'coon before he went in.

"It was Adam Conway from over at Falling Water. He's been down in Alabama, and now he's got leave to come home, or anyhow he took leave," Mr. Brabson was saying. "He come by about noon and told Sallie Jean he seen Jethro yesterday morning in Bridgeport. Jethro's plumb put out. He figured to do some real fighting when he joined up, but they've made him a wagon driver."

"Well, I'm glad," said Mrs. Brabson. "I know somebody's got to do the fighting, and a body ought not to want her son to be spared over and above other mothers' sons. But I can't help being glad he ain't out there shooting and being shot at."

"Well, of course, it don't mean he's out of danger," Mr. Brabson warned her gravely. "I reckon a heap of boys been killed driving wagons. Of course it ain't as bad as being right in the fighting, by a long shot."

Oh, I reckon a heap of Yankee wagon drivers are going to meet their maker this day, Chris thought as he stood his rifle up in the corner. *I reckon most nigh all of them will be dead by the time the Confederates get through with them.*

He stood there a minute by the table. That supply train was coming from Bridgeport. Jethro might well be one of those wagon drivers. A little cold sliver of fear went darting through Chris. Right this minute Silas was running to fetch the Southern soldiers. And when the troops came, they weren't going to find out if one of the drivers was Jethro Brabson. They were just going to kill them all.

Chris raised his eyes to his mother's face. He'd as good as murdered his own brother. He might as well have done it with his own hands as to do it this way. And someday they'd all know, his mammy and his pappy and Sallie Jean—all of them would know how he'd been the one to betray Jethro and lay him in his bury box.

He sprang toward the door suddenly. He'd go after Silas and stop him!

"Where you headed, Chris?" cried Mrs. Brabson. "I aim to have supper on the table in just a little spell."

"I . . . I got to go," called Chris through the door. "I forgot something. I'll be back."

He ran then, as hard as he could, to keep from having to say anything else, and to keep himself from hearing if they called him. When he stopped to get his breath, he was too far away to hear. The shadows of the trees stretched out long beside him. He'd have to make haste. He'd have to get after Silas quick.

But which way would he go? He had no notion where Silas went to tell the Rebel generals what he knew. Would it be east or west? Or maybe south? He didn't know, and there wasn't any way he could find out. He tried to think. But it wasn't any use.

He gritted his teeth in anger at himself. Oh, whatever had made him do this thing in the first place? Whatever had made him think he wanted to be a spy? There was little hope for Jethro now. By tomorrow morning he would be dead, lying beside a wagon in Sequatchie Valley. Chris and Pappy would have to go down there and fetch his body home. "Oh, Jethro," Chris moaned. "I never went to do hurt to you. I swear I never."

Unless . . . unless he could get down in the valley tonight and warn his brother the Rebels were coming. They wouldn't attack the wagon train till daylight surely, so there was time. But could he find Jethro's wagon among all those hundreds of wagons?

I got to try, he told himself. *There ain't nothing I can do but try.*

He began to run again. He wouldn't go the road. He would take the path. It was rocky and steep, but it would get him down the mountain in half the time it would take on the road. He reached the edge of the mountain and stopped for a minute to look down.

In the red sunset light he could still see the long row of wagons below, and here and there a campfire, like a star reflected in the dusky valley. He took a deep breath and plunged down the mountainside.

12

Chris crouched at the edge of a thicket, peering out from among the cow-itch vines at the Yankees moving about their campfire. He'd seen a heap of Yankee soldiers on the mountaintop, but he balked at walking right smack in among them.

He watched one of the soldiers go to a wagon and lift out a big wooden box. The man returned to the fire and dropped the box carelessly on the ground. Chris could see the letters on the side plain as could be, but he doubted that BREAD was inside. What kind of bread could come squashed up in such a box? Whatever it was, it couldn't possibly be fitten to eat.

The soldier knocked open the top of the box and held up a square brown solid-looking object. "What have we here?" he cried. "Hardtack, boys. And it ain't changed a bit. Good for hammering nails or using as shoe soles or even melting down for bullets.

But not much for eating, I'll say." He dropped it back in the box and it hit with a loud clunk.

Another soldier walked over to the fire with a long-handled spoon and stirred something in a pot. "Stew's ready," he said. "Let's eat, Sarge."

The other soldiers crowded around, holding out metal plates and snatching up the hardtack. One soldier ate from a black skillet, another out of his cup.

Chris shifted uneasily. He couldn't stay here all night watching these Yanks. Much as he dreaded to, he had to step in there among them and ask for Jethro. It was the only thing he knew to do.

He pushed aside the vines, but still he hung back. When the Feds looked at him, would they see how much he despised them? Would they know this was a Rebel lad who'd betrayed them into the hands of the Confederate army?

Go on, he told himself. *It ain't as bad as letting the mules loose. You know it ain't. Go on!*

Slowly, anxiously, Chris walked through the stubble toward the fire, trying to make up his mind what he would say. *I'll just be mannerly and say "Good evening" first off,* he thought. But he didn't get a chance. One of the wagoners looked up and saw him before Chris had so much as opened his mouth.

"What do you want, boy?" the man growled angrily. His voice sounded harsh and flat.

Chris gulped, looking about miserably. Finally he managed to speak. "I'm a-looking for a feller by the name of Brabson. Jethro Brabson." He added uncertainly, "You ain't seen him, have you?"

"Never heard of him," said the soldier sharply, going back to his food.

The other soldiers sitting around the fire looked up at Chris. To him their faces all looked dark and hostile. None of them spoke a word. Chris's lip curled. Oh, he hated Yankees. He might have reckoned on them not being friendly or helpful or even decent.

"I thank ye kindly," he said stiffly and got away into the dark as quick as he could.

He stumbled on to the next campfire. He was mad all the way through, and he shouted out, bold and loud, before he reached the light, "Does any of you know a feller named Jethro Brabson?"

The soldiers looked up in surprise. "Who's there?" one asked.

Chris stepped forward where the light fell right on him. Let all these Yanks see him good. Maybe they could tell he was a Reb just by looking at him. And maybe they could tell he was a spy. He didn't care. He hated them all, and he wasn't scared a trifle.

"What's that name again?" the soldier asked.

"Jethro Brabson," Chris repeated.

Two or three soldiers shook their heads. But one of them spoke up, just as Chris was leaving. "Hey, boy," he called. "You from around here?"

Chris's mouth went dry. So they *could* tell he was a Confederate. He tensed, ready to run. Nobody made a move toward him, and he stood his ground. "I come from up on the mountain," he said as bravely as he could.

"Well, some of the wagons on down the road got drivers from these parts," the soldier told him. "They may know the man you're looking for."

Chris was so surprised he couldn't answer at first. Maybe this wasn't really a flinty-hearted Yankee, this man who'd done him a kindness, who had tried politely to help him out.

"I'm m-m-mighty much obliged," he stammered at last and hurried off.

He went a good piece down the road and asked again. No, the men didn't know Jethro. They didn't know any drivers who came from around here. Chris swallowed his misery and ran on, in and out among canvas-topped wagons, funny-looking Yankee wagons with the back wheels bigger than the front ones.

One whole long string of wagons had AMMUNITION printed on the canvas sides. Chris got away from there fast. *There ought to be enough powder in there to blow up Walden's Ridge,* he thought grimly.

The soldiers around these wagons looked different from the others. Chris slowed, watching them. They were more sober and wearier-looking than the wagon drivers. A row of horses was tied to a fence, and near them a soldier slept with a coat and several tow sacks piled over him. His feet stuck out from under all the covers. He had holes in his stockings, and Chris could see the dirty skin gleam through. The man's boots were there beside him, and a sword and pistol, handy for quick grabbing. Chris went on, stumbling over a saddle. This was the cavalry, and there wasn't a bit of use looking for Jethro here.

Many of the soldiers tried to be helpful. One remembered talking to a driver named Brabson. He thought he was in one of the first wagons. Chris tramped back up to the head of the train. But nobody in the first wagons knew Jethro. Chris ran back the way he had come.

He climbed over wagon tongues and over rickety fences, trotted past stacked rifles. He crossed pastures among quietly grazing mules, lurched through the mud of a cornfield, beat back and forth across the road a hundred times, trying to get to every campfire.

He had stopped asking for Jethro now. That took time, and time was getting mighty short. He would run up to a fire, glance hurriedly around at the men's faces, and then leave. *Jethro!* he cried desperately in his heart. He had to find Jethro.

But at last he was winded. He couldn't drag himself another step. He leaned against a tailgate and pressed his hot, sweaty face against a cold strip of metal. He'd get his breath back and then push on. He didn't dare stop longer than that. If Jethro got killed, Chris would never again hold up his head. He would always and forever be bowed down with the pain of it.

Over there the wagoners were singing loud enough to wake the dead. Above the voices he heard a fiddle, its music drifting thinly out through the night to him. Jethro could play the fiddle. Maybe this was Jethro playing. Chris headed toward the fire, but it was some other fiddler.

He rubbed his eyes and plodded on to the next fire. Three men were crouched together playing cards. But Jethro wasn't one of them. And he wasn't among those standing around a man with a guitar. Another soldier was sitting on a log. Chris shifted to see his face and staggered a little as he turned. The soldier on the log stared back at him.

"Hey, boy! Come here."

Chris gazed at the soldier stupidly. He didn't move. The soldier looked at him sharply.

"What's wrong with you, boy?" he asked kindly. "This here is the second time tonight you been here. First you come running up all wild-eyed to look around and then tear off. And now you come looking like you been chewed up and spat out. You in trouble?"

"I'm a-looking for my brother, Jethro Brabson," Chris answered. Twice! He'd been to this camp twice! And maybe to a heap more the same way. He must have wasted a power of time doing that.

"Well, sit down and rest. You look all tuckered," the man told him.

"No," cried Chris desperately. "I got to find Jethro."

"Well, he ain't going no place. He'll still be right where he is now when you go to look for him," the soldier said, smiling. He had a funny little beard like a goat's, and it waggled every time he said something. "Sit down and I'll get you some coffee."

Reluctantly Chris sat down. Right away he knew it was a mistake. *My legs are so beat out I won't never get them to stand up again,* he thought miserably.

The soldier threw what was left in his tin mug over his shoulder. He got up and went to the fire.

Chris watched him. He was a big man, dressed in faded, torn clothes. There wasn't a button on his coat, and his shoes were worn through at the toe. Folks always said Yankee soldiers had nothing but fine clean uniforms, but Chris could see that wasn't so. He took the mug of coffee with mumbled thanks. It was scalding hot and mighty bitter in spite of the big spoons of sugar the soldier had put in. Anyway, it was something to put in his innards.

The soldier sat beside Chris on the log. "Sorry we ain't got nothing left to eat."

A wagoner squatting beside the pot of coffee turned. "I was along here just last week and seen two deer break across the road. Too bad it didn't happen this evening. I got a gun with me now, and we'd have had roast venison for supper."

"You mean Captain Foster would have had roast venison," jeered another wagoner. "If you was to fire a shot, he'd be here before the deer hit the ground and commandeer it as officers' property."

"Captain Foster's quick, but I'm a streak of lightning," answered the soldier beside the pot. "I'd have that deer skinned, roasted, and eaten before he got here. All Captain Foster would get would be a smell of meat."

The soldier with the goatee said suddenly, "If I was just home where I could get a buck lined up in my sights, I would feel a whole lot better." He sighed. "This is the time of year I like best. I ain't missed going hunting in the fall since I was knee-high to a duck." He paused and added, "Till now I haven't."

Chris glanced around at the wagoners in surprise. He hadn't known Yankees ever went hunting. He thought they all lived in big towns with hardly a blade of grass or a tree anywhere near, much less any game. He hadn't known they could love hunting the same as he did.

"Put some more wood on that fire," called out a fat soldier. "My mama told me to always keep my feet warm."

"Throw your head on," answered the soldier behind Chris. "That's wood and you don't ever use it anyhow."

Chris couldn't help grinning. He didn't want to laugh at a Yankee joke, but it slipped out. He took a quick swallow of coffee. He'd have to go on looking for Jethro now. He finished the cup and set it on the log.

The soldier with the goatee jumped up. "I think I'll get us something to eat," he said. "Ginger snaps, maybe. Would you like some?"

"What's them?" Chris asked. They didn't sound so good to him.

"Little cakes," the soldier replied. "The sutler sells them. His wagon's up the road about a quarter of a mile. He sells all kinds of pies and cakes, but ginger snaps is best."

He felt in his pocket for his money. "You wait here now and I'll be right back." He went off into the dark.

Chris wanted to say he couldn't wait. He didn't want any Yankee doing him a favor, tramping around through the dark to buy him goodies. Besides, he had to go after Jethro. But it was too late; the soldier was gone. And Chris was too bone-tired to run after him.

Chris stared around. Here he was all by himself among the enemy. They didn't seem so wicked. It was true some of them had a queer way of talking. But for the most part, they seemed friendly-hearted.

I reckon they ain't real Yankee soldiers, Chris thought. *Just wagoners.*

A soldier on the other side of the fire was tuning his guitar.

A wagoner moved over beside Chris. "Have one of these here apples," he said, holding out a hatful. He was a young man, not much more than seventeen or eighteen, Chris figured.

I reckon he stole them from some Southerner any-

way, Chris told himself, and he took one and ate it hungrily.

Four of the soldiers began to sing. Chris listened in surprise. The music was like nothing he'd ever heard before. But oh, it was pretty. Such a gay tune and the men's voices seemed to each take different parts, break away from each other, yet come back together again in a way he didn't know people could sing. On the mountain folks just sang a ballad straight out.

The young soldier chewed gloomily. "You live around here?" he asked, when the song was over. Chris nodded. "You're lucky," the Yankee went on. "If I was this close to my home, I'd leave this army and it wouldn't never see me again."

Chris was startled. "How come?" he wanted to know. "Don't you like the army?" He'd thought all Yankees were dying to come south and whip the daylights out of the Rebels.

The soldier frowned. "Oh, the army ain't too bad. And I joined up of my own free will. It wasn't right to let the Union break up, you know," he explained. "But the thing is, I'm needed at home. My daddy died this past summer, and my brothers is all married and gone off. There ain't nobody to look after the home-place but me. My mother, she can't take care of the stock and all, by herself. She needs help. I guess the hay will have to rot in the fields, and then she won't have nothing to feed the cattle this winter. . . ."

He broke off and stared sadly at his apple for a moment. Then he flung it angrily out into the night. "I wrote Mr. Lincoln a letter and I said please just let me go home long enough to get the hay in." He sighed. "But I don't reckon he ever got the letter, and here I be."

Chris watched the soldier out of the corner of his eye. He was glad he wasn't the one far from home with such things happening to his folks. It would be mortal hard to know your pappy was dead and your mammy knee-deep in trouble and you couldn't help one mite.

He yawned and moved a little bit farther from the fire. He was getting sleepy. That must be what was the matter with him, feeling sorry for Yankees. If this boy had stayed home where he belonged, not joined the army to come sticking his nose in Southern folks' affairs, he wouldn't be in trouble now.

The soldiers were singing again. It was a song sad and mournful as a turtledove's call. Chris noticed two or three of the group looked woeful enough to wring your heart. The young soldier's eyes filled with tears.

"Don't sing no more of them gloomy songs," yelled the fat soldier. "I'm too far from home. Sing something lively or I'll bust that guitar."

Chris's eyes clouded with weariness. He shook his head. He couldn't let himself go to sleep.

The goateed soldier came back from the sutler's tent with a bag in his hand. He handed Chris a round flat cake. "Ginger snaps," he said, placing the bag between them. "Take all you want."

The cake was sweet and chewy and fiery to taste. At first Chris didn't think he liked it, but then he decided he did. He ate three or four, sitting there listening to the soldiers' talk and the singing. He had to struggle to keep awake. Half the time he hardly knew where he was or why he was there.

Jethro, he thought once. *I got to find Jethro.*

He stood up and walked away into the dark, and then his head jerked and he woke up and knew he had dreamed. He was still there by the Yankee campfire with half a ginger snap in his hand.

Chris didn't remember going back to sleep. But a little later he felt himself being lifted up. "We'll stow him in my wagon for the night," said a soldier's voice.

"Wonder what he's doing here anyway?" asked another.

I'd ought to tell them, Chris thought sleepily.

Them two Yankees been good to me. They ain't wicked and hateful. And I ought to warn them about the Rebels coming.

He *would* tell them. In just a minute as soon as he got his eyes open properly, he'd tell them.

But the next thing he heard was shooting. A mule brayed piteously and a man screamed. Chris jumped up, shaking and scared. It took him a minute to remember where he was. He looked out over the tailgate. There were men running everywhere, and all sorts of noise and confusion.

Four soldiers on horseback galloped toward him. Rebs! The soldiers' coats were gray! The Confederate troops had come! The attack had started and he hadn't warned anybody, and he had no idea where Jethro was!

13

Chris waved at the Rebel horsemen to let them know he was one of them. He hadn't planned on being here when the fight started, but he reckoned they could see he wasn't an enemy soldier.

The horsemen came on toward the wagon. Then one of the men raised his pistol. He lifted himself above the saddle, almost standing upright in his stirrups, and aimed over the horse's head smack at Chris.

Chris waved frantically. Couldn't they see him? Suddenly it came over him that these riders had no way of telling he was a Southerner, half-hidden as he was by the tailgate. He was in a Yankee wagon with Yankee soldiers, and that was enough for them. Yankees might smile and wave all they pleased, but they got shot just the same.

"Don't! Don't shoot!" he screamed out, panic-stricken.

The rider fired, and a bullet crashed into the tailgate. Chris looked down in horror at the jagged hole, at the great splinter ripped from the wood when the ball came out. It was not a hand's span from where he knelt. It made him sick to think how that lead bullet could have whammed into his ribs and on through his chest.

He glanced up to find the pistol still aimed right at him and the cavalrymen coming on. He cowered back inside the wagon, out of sight. He didn't hear the second shot, but a hole suddenly appeared in the canvas over his head. Chris yelled like an Indian and burrowed down among the sacks of potatoes.

He could hear the driver bawling and cursing at the mules. The wagon started off with a jerk, going fast across the rough field, bumping and swaying from side to side. The bags of potatoes rolled about, and he had to fight his way out from under them. But he couldn't stay on top of them. He was thrown helplessly back and forth, slamming up against the tailgate till his body ached and his head swam.

There was a great jolt, and Chris bounced high and came down against the wooden side. He grabbed it and clung there, battered and bruised, pushing at the bags as they slid toward him. The wagon trembled and shook so he could hardly hold on.

Suddenly the wagon swerved and tilted up on

two wheels. The potatoes fell away from under him. He gripped the plank siding with all his strength. The wagon lurched forward, leaning more and more. Chris hollered, scrabbling wildly for a firmer grip. Then the wagon crashed over on its side and Chris shot through the canvas top.

He threw up his arms to protect his face and never even knew when he went through the canvas. He hit the ground half on his shoulder and rolled over to his back hard enough to jar his teeth loose. He lay there breathless and dizzy, with potatoes all around him.

The mules brayed in terror. Chris got up as quick as he could. The wagon tongue had broken and gone right through one of the mules. The beast kicked feebly and then was still. The others floundered among the twisted traces, snorting and rearing. The front one broke loose and began to lope off. The driver grabbed for the flapping traces and missed. He looked over his shoulder and then sprinted after the mule.

A gun cracked and the driver gave a little jump in the air and then fell. Chris jerked around. There was a horseman almost right behind him. He had his pistol ready. He was so close he couldn't miss.

Chris shrank back against the wagon. *Don't shoot!* he wanted to yell. *I ain't no Yankee soldier; don't shoot!* But his voice was frozen somewhere down inside his chest. He couldn't speak.

The rider slowed his horse. "Git on home to your mammy, boy!" he cried in a deep voice. "Git on!" He gestured threateningly with the pistol and jerked his horse around. He raked his spurs across the animal's side and rode off.

Chris moved away from the wagon and started across the field running. He'd have to find some safe place to hide till all this shooting was over. He stopped short. A Yankee came sprinting toward him. His mouth was open wide in terror and his arms were stretched helplessly out in front of him. Right behind him raced a gray-coated cavalryman. The Rebel dashed up beside him and raised his sword high above his head. The runner screamed as the sword slashed down into his neck and shoulder.

Chris saw the quick wave of blood, and the man's head fell forward. With a sick shudder he turned and fled the other way. When he reached the edge of the field, he pushed on into the high weeds, scurrying among the dried stalks as fast as he could.

Something hard rolled from under his foot, and he fell. Getting to his knees, he saw it was a man's leg. Fearfully he stood up and looked at the soldier's face. It was the goateed Federal who'd bought him the ginger snaps. He lay in the weeds with his mouth in a twisted grimace and his eyes staring sightlessly at the purple-flowered ironweeds. A great dark hole gaped in his throat and chest.

Chris trembled all over. "I as good as killed him," he whispered. "I could of warned him, and he'd of got away."

He staggered off to the fencerow and crouched down in some sumac. The fighting seemed heavier than ever. He didn't want to look, but he was scared not to. He peered out, but all he saw was a Confederate soldier shooting down mules as fast as he could point a gun at them. With every shot Chris flinched. It seemed like the whole world had gone crazy.

He shut his eyes and put his shaking hands over his ears. *I done all this*, he thought in agony. *This here was all my doing. It was me sent Silas running to get the Rebs.*

But he hadn't thought about it being like this. He'd thought about being a hero and helping out the Confederacy. He hadn't known about things like the goateed driver getting killed, and the mules screaming, and the awful way men looked when they set out to kill each other.

It ain't true, he told himself. *It ain't true, none of it ain't. I'll open my eyes in a minute and won't none of it be true.*

He opened his eyes suddenly, but it was true. He was still crouched there in the sumac. The fighting was still going on. The picture of destruction was burned forever into his mind. He'd never forget it.

He sat there a long time, half-stupefied. There was a sudden great blast, and the earth shook. Chris knew what it was. They were blowing up the ammunition wagons. The fighting must be almost over.

He crawled along the fencerow and out of the sumac. The end of the world had come, it seemed like. It was dark as night, here in the middle of the morning. Smoke and dust rolled over the road toward him in thick, black clouds. The sound of gunfire was far off, but the crackle of fire was all around. Everywhere there were burning wagons.

Another wagon of ammunition exploded with a roar and a terrible flash. Chris began to cough from the sour smoke. A Rebel horseman loomed over him with a torch in his hand. Chris leaped aside and fell to his knees, and the horseman rushed past.

Maybe I'm dead and in hell, Chris thought. The very air about him was red now, a strange, hazy blood-red. Flames leaped up before him, flicked out, and seemed to close in around him.

He had to get away from here and go home. There was nothing he could do here to undo the terrible thing he had done. Likely they wouldn't want him at home, but he didn't have any place else to go.

He got to his feet and went blindly forward, crossed the road, leaped a ditch into the dry grass. There was another loud blast, and a piece of wagon wheel whistled through the air and spun into the ground near him. He kept going around dead mules and fallen soldiers. Ahead of him through the twisting rolls of smoke he saw a burning wagon collapse into the weeds. Flames spouted out in every direction and licked along the grass toward him.

He headed back toward the road and walked down it to a bare field. The air was clearer here, and he could see a bunch of little scrubby trees just ahead. He ran forward and slipped in among the saplings. He grasped a trunk, and the feel of the rough bark under his hand seemed to him the first real thing that had happened to him today.

"Boy!" somebody whispered in a harsh voice. "Hey, boy!"

Chris drew in his breath sharply. Who was in here with him? "What you want?" he snarled, and he was surprised at how ugly and sharp his voice sounded.

"Come over here," the voice said more loudly.

Reluctantly Chris obeyed. It was the young soldier who had given him the apple. He was sitting propped against a tree, his uniform torn and his face blackened. There was a big ugly red place in his chest that he kept dabbing at with a piece of blood-soaked cloth. He grinned faintly at Chris.

"There ain't anything like a good fight for starting the day off right, is there?" he wanted to know.

Chris didn't smile. "You want help?" he asked. "I ain't seen nobody around, but I'll look for somebody to help you."

The soldier shook his head. "Naw, I don't guess there's anybody left alive by now to help me," he answered. "Anyway, water's what I need bad."

Chris stared at the wounded man. He wanted to get away from here as fast as he could. It would take time to hunt for a creek and bring water back here. But he owed this soldier that much. He had to do it. *It was me got him hurt anyway*, he thought.

"I'll git it for you," he told the soldier.

He ran back the way he'd come. He remembered a pool of water in a ditch somewhere. That would be the quickest. The edge of the field was lined with dead mules, and on the road beyond stood a long row of burned and smoking wagons. He could hardly bear to look.

And then he came on a gray figure face down in the mud. He gritted his teeth together till his jaws ached. It was his fault his own country's soldier was lying here dead, that all these men of both sides were killed, and the mules and the horses, and the wagons and ammunition blown up.

I should have spoke out last night and said the Rebs were coming, he thought wretchedly. *There wasn't any of them men hateful the way I reckoned they would be. I could have saved them anyway.*

But even late last night he reckoned it was too late. The road was so crowded with wagons and animals they couldn't have gotten away. There'd have been a fight. Where he'd done wrong was to tell Silas in the first place. Whatever made him think spying was such a fine thing anyway?

He ran past a blazing wagon, beating the flying sparks off his shirt. Jethro had joined the Union army, and Jethro wasn't hateful and wicked. He was kindhearted and good-natured, quick to do a good turn for other folks. Chris groaned to himself. Why hadn't he stopped to think some other Yanks might be kindhearted folks, too?

He found a small branch and then a coffeepot to fetch the water in. He filled the pot and turned to go when he saw something moving around an overturned wagon. It was a Confederate soldier, pawing through the sacks and broken boxes.

He walked over to him, watching the man hold up something in his hands and take big bites out of it. The man nodded to him but kept right on eating. Chris reckoned this must have been the sutler's wagon. Breadstuffs and sweets lay here and there on the ground, even some ginger snaps.

"Help yourself," cried the Confederate. "It ain't hurt none, just trampled a little."

Chris shook his head. The soldier shrugged. "Tastes mighty fine. First sweet thing I've had to eat since Heck was a pup." He stopped and grabbed up a fried pie. "Where you from?" he asked the boy.

"Up on the mountain," Chris answered.

"What you doing here?"

Chris looked uneasy. "I . . . I come to see the fight," he stammered.

The soldier laughed. "Warn't it a fine one? That's how General Wheeler's going to treat the Yanks all the way across Tennessee. We started out three days ago, and this here is the best fight we've had."

Three days ago! Chris almost dropped the pot. Then the Rebel cavalry hadn't come because of him! They'd been on their way to Sequatchie Valley before he'd even known about the wagon train, long before he'd told the news to Silas!

He felt suddenly as though he'd been toting a load of lead on his shoulders and somebody had come up behind him and lifted it off. He wished the soldier good luck and turned away. He walked on with his heavy pot, but it hardly seemed to weigh anything now.

The ground shook with another explosion. The Rebels must have found some more wagons full of powder up on the road up the mountainside. It looked as though the Rebs would try to take all that ammunition with them if they were going to fight their way across Tennessee, instead of wasting it that way. But oh, at least it wasn't any of his doing. He wasn't the one who had brought about all this death and destruction.

He had to look around a spell before he found his way back to the soldier. The Yank was sitting with his eyes closed when Chris got back, and for just a minute Chris thought he was dead. But he looked up when Chris crouched by him.

"I come as quick as I could," Chris told him.

"I know you did," the soldier whispered. He sat up and reached for the pot, groaning as he moved. He drank deeply and then sat the pot down close to him. "Thanks," he said at last. "That was a good turn."

In a few minutes he seemed to feel better. "I guess you was surprised to be in a battle," he said. "We was all kind of taken off guard. We didn't have enough cavalry or infantry soldiers along with us for such a big lot of wagons." He looked at Chris. "What was you doing there anyway?"

"I was looking for my brother," Chris answered slowly. "He's a wagoner. We heard he was down in Bridgeport, and then when I seen all these wagons, I figured he might be in one."

The soldier nodded. He picked up the pot. "How long has he been in the army?" he asked curiously and took another drink.

"He just left home four days ago," answered Chris.

The soldier laughed and wiped his mouth. He held his chest a moment with his hand. "He's safe as houses, then," he answered. "He'll be learning how to march and drill and such as that for a time to come. It'll be a month or two before he gets in a wagon!"

Chris stared at him. Then every single thing he'd done had turned out different than he'd planned. He hadn't been a spy or brought the Confederates or come anywhere near saving Jethro. He didn't know whether to laugh or to cry. All he'd done was eat ginger snaps and fetch this boy some water.

He stood up. "I'm a-going now," he said to the soldier. "If I see anybody that can help you, I'll tell 'em where you are."

The boy grinned. "I'll be all right," he said.

"I'm too tough to die. Anyway the Medical Corps will be around pretty soon to take care of me. But thanks for the water. You're a friend indeed."

"Good-bye," said Chris, and he set out.

Some of the haze had blown away, and he could see the mountain plain. He left Anderson Road and looked for the path up the mountain. He reckoned his folks would be worried about him, and he was sorry.

I reckon they'll be mad, and I can't blame 'em, he thought. *But I ain't no spy. At least I ain't no spy!*

14

Chris was almost to the top of the mountain. But even up here he couldn't get away from the battle. The smoke and dust rolled and roiled among the trees. The sharp scent of powder was half-stifling.

I reckon even if I couldn't smell this smoke, thought Chris, *even if there wasn't a leaf changed from what it was when I left here yesterday, it would look different to me. I'm different from what I was yesterday. Won't nothing look just like it used to, not to me it won't ever again.*

He put out his hand to break off a sourwood leaf to chew. But his fingers were powder-blackened and grimy, and he drew them back. It didn't seem right to touch anything with these hands. When he got home, he'd get Mammy to heat him some water and he'd wash in the big black kettle. He'd get a heap of lye soap and scrub good and put on clean clothes. He'd do that first off.

But what was he going to tell them at home? He could tell them he'd gone to see Jethro. It wouldn't be a lie, not a real one. He didn't much think they'd believe that was all there was to it.

He was too tired to make up a lie anyway. If the truth was what he had to tell them, then he'd tell them the truth. And after that he'd forget it as quick as he could. He didn't want to think any more about it. He couldn't pretend it hadn't happened, but at least he could put it out of his head.

At the top of the path he turned and looked back. The green and gold valley was filled with smoke. He couldn't see anything except here and there a fire towered up and glowed through the haze. He shivered and ran on.

He hadn't gone far when he came around a bend in the trail and saw his father standing there. Mr. Brabson walked toward him quickly. His eyes blazed, and when he came up to Chris, he took his son by the shoulder and shook him hard.

"Where you been?" he cried hoarsely. "Don't you know we been half-crazy looking for you? Are you addled? Ain't you got enough sense to come home?"

Chris gasped. His pappy shook him like a dog shakes a rat. "I . . . I been down yonder," he said, panting.

But Mr. Brabson didn't seem to hear. "You didn't come home and you didn't come home and your mammy got to fretting. She figured you was at Silas's, and she walked over there herself. And Silas said he ain't seen you . . ."

"Silas!" screamed Chris. "Silas was home?"

"He was home then," said Mr. Brabson, surprised. "Him and me spent a good part of the night out looking for you. Your mammy made sure you was hurt bad and couldn't get back home."

Chris's legs gave way under him, and he sat down in the dust. Silas wasn't a spy. He hadn't even gone out of his cabin. He'd lied, saying he was setting out to tell the Rebs about the wagon train. It hadn't made any real difference in what happened, but it seemed to Chris to be the meanest trick anybody had played on him ever. He shut his eyes tight and squeezed back the scalding tears.

He wiped his face on his sleeve and gulped. A red and black beetle climbed out of one of the wagon ruts, and he poked it back with his toe. His father put a gentle hand on his shoulder.

"What ails you, Chris?" he asked. "What you been up to?"

Chris told him then. He told him about the shirt and how he hated Yankees and how he'd let the mules out of the pen. And about seeing the wagons and how he'd told Silas, because he thought Silas was a spy. And then the awful minute when he'd heard about Jethro and thought he'd killed his own brother.

"I went down there and I couldn't find Jethro nowhere, Pappy," Chris said quickly. "I didn't know about how he had to learn soldiering and wouldn't be in a wagon train for a long spell yet. But anyway . . ." He broke off. "Pappy, I reckon a Yankee ain't so all-fired mean as I thought. Some of them was real fine. There was one feller liked to go hunting just like me, only he's dead now. But he bought me some ginger snaps, little sweet cakes they was." He put his hand in his pocket, and there was still half of a ginger snap there, a little crumbly but still eatable. He'd give it to Leah.

"It come over me I didn't hate them fellers even if they did come down here where they don't belong," he went on. "I aimed to tell them about the Rebs coming, but I . . . I went to sleep. And when I woke up, it was too late. The cavalry was already there, killing and burning and . . ." He stopped and looked away, biting his lip, shaking a little in spite of himself.

His father didn't say anything for a few minutes. "But it couldn't of been your doing," he declared finally. "Silas ain't no spy. He never went nowhere to carry the word. Silas is just an old lighthead who likes to act big and stir up trouble any which a way he can."

"I know it," muttered Chris. "I know it wasn't my doing. But I feel like it was."

"There ain't no call for you to feel that way, Chris," said Mr. Brabson firmly. "Come on now. We got to git home and tell your mammy you're safe."

But still Chris sat there.

"And you got to have some food and rest and get washed," went on his father. "Surely there ain't any sense in you mourning around about what you done. Like I told you before, war is the worst thing that can happen to folks, and the reason is it makes most everybody do things they shouldn't. Maybe when you git growed up, folks can think of a better way to settle their differences than shooting at each other. Seems like they ought to try mighty hard to anyway. But if I was you, I wouldn't take all the credit for them not having done it so far."

Chris stood up then and nodded slowly.

Mr. Brabson took him by the shoulders and pushed him gently along the path. "There ain't no use you blaming yourself for the whole thing. What you got to blame yourself for is acting foolish."

"I reckon I been foolish," Chris said soberly. "I should of knowed Silas wasn't no spy."

Mr. Brabson stopped short. "What you should of knowed," he exclaimed severely, "was that a man can believe the Union ought to stay in one piece and still be a good decent man that don't deserve to be killed."

Chris nodded miserably.

"A body can favor secession and the Confederacy if that's the way he feels about it," Mr. Brabson went on. "But it don't mean he can go around doing any fool thing he takes a notion. I reckon Silas was back of a lot of what you did. And Silas is as giddy-acting as they come. Looky yonder!"

Chris looked. Slowly, gracefully, three young bucks made their way across the trail and into the woods.

"Now where was they yesterday when I had my rifle and a heap of powder and lead?" Chris asked indignantly.

Mr. Brabson chuckled. "They was laying low. But you'll get 'em yet. We'll need deer meat this winter, a heap of it. There'll be time aplenty for you to go hunting." He rubbed his chin thoughtfully. "I'm a good hand at curing skins. And your mammy can sew a fine seam. I reckon you could shoot enough deer to make you a whole suit of deer-hide clothes."

Chris looked around at his father. "For a fact, Pappy?"

Mr. Brabson nodded. "For a fact," he answered.

Chris kicked at a pine cone and looked about him. This was his mountaintop and he loved it. There were deer to be hunted and things to be done and a life to live here. The war might last a long time, and when it was over, things would be changed. Nothing would be quite the same as it had been, not ever.

But it wouldn't matter. There would still be good things to do, hunting and teasing Leah and talking to his pappy and listening to his mammy tell tales.

They turned and went along through the fields. Chris could see the house now. His heart gave a bump. It was such a fine cabin. He'd come home safe to it in spite of going to war and spying and all the things he'd done. And it wouldn't make any difference to his mammy and his pappy. They loved him no matter what he thought about the war.

Suddenly he couldn't wait to get home. They had almost reached the edge of the clearing, and Chris began to run.